Acknowledgments

Thanks to Julie for putting up with Red working through the night and to Jan for her support during 'book club' nights.

Also, thanks to Emmy Griffiths for her input during the editing process.

This book is dedicated to Gordon Watkins and all members of the Armed Forces.

Let the imagineering begin

Red Mckenzie

Chapter 1

Billy

Little did Billy Waring realise how his life was going to change when he uncovered the cold, almost grey, bones after a day of clearing the leaves from his grandmother's orchard.

Autumn was upon the world. The leaves were changing colour; bronze; yellow; fiery-red and lime green. They fell to the ground one after the other as they gave up their desperate struggle to hang on by a thread; floating to the ground and bidding farewell to the fruit trees they had helped nurture through the summer months.

The two Tamworth pigs, which Billy called Ethel and Nancy, were busy eating the windfalls before the fruit could turn to brown sludge.

"Makes the pork taste better." Uncle Albert used to bellow.

Billy, who had heard himself being described as a "well rounded boy" – a description he still hadn't fathomed out the meaning of – was about to celebrate his ninth birthday the following day; 12th October 1953. He was wearing his favourite navy blue dungarees that sported a tear in the knee; a hole that grew bigger day by day. Each time he stepped into them his foot would go half way down and shoot straight through the ever increasing hole. He was pretty sure that if anyone had been watching him he would have looked a funny sight hopping about like a cat on a hot tin roof as he tried not to lose his balance and fall flat on his bottom.

His black pit boots were also wearing thin in the soles but he would not wear anything else. The man in the shop where Billy had bought them from had told him that the boots belonged to a World War Two infantryman. Billy thought this was wonderful and wondered what stories the boots could tell if they could talk. In truth, Billy's imagination would always run wild when he thought about the Second World War.

As Billy piled up the leaves his mind was beginning to wander on to the war when he was suddenly alerted to a snuffling sound at the end of his boots. Spooked by the sensation of something brushing against his feet he spun around and ran as fast as he could out of the orchard. When he glanced over his shoulder to look back he realised it had only been Ethel. She had been trying to move Billy's foot as he had been standing on a particularly juicy apple that she had wanted to eat as part of her potato and apple diet; and nothing was going to stop her getting at it!

Billy returned to the orchard and finished raking the leaves. It was starting to go dark so he decided it was time to pack up. He put the last of the fallen leaves he'd piled up on the compost heap and then gathered up his tools before taking them the short distance across the orchard to the tool shed.

As he opened the door to the shed he had the familiar feeling he always got that he was entering another world. The musty smell of old sack cloth mixed in with the not unpleasant smell of creosote invaded his nostrils. It was quite a big shed and Billy regarded it as a treasure trove of mysteries. There were tools in there from a by-gone age which had rusted with time but that no-one felt the urge to dispose of. Boxes of various sizes were strewn around containing goodness knows what and that Billy had promised himself, despite being told not to by his grandmother, he would investigate one day.

He stood there for a moment in the entrance, rake and brush in hand, taking in this wonderland before sighing deeply. He trundled over to the far corner and inserted the rake into the two rusty nails strategically hammered into the side of the shed to allow its safe storage. However, as Billy went to place the brush in its rightful place one of the nails, finally corroded by the rust, gave way and the rake came crashing off its resting place, catching a pile of boxes as it did so.

Billy watched in awe as, in slow motion, the tower of boxes came tumbling down. He leapt across the shed in a vain attempt to keep the boxes upright. As they hit the floor, a flurry of dust was sent shooting into the air.

"Darn it!" Billy muttered under his breath before sneezing.

With an air of resignation, he started to reconstruct the tower. As he did so, he came across a box probably just big enough to keep his football in. It was filled with straw which, having been disturbed by the fall, was now bursting out of the top.

Billy couldn't resist the urge to look inside. What he found in there had his eyes popping out of his head. It was a human skull!

Billy stared at it for a while working up the courage to take it out of the box. He kept telling himself that it surely couldn't be a real one. It must have been a stage prop like the one they used in that awful play he was made to watch by his parents or even like the one on the skeleton hanging in his school science lab. No way was it real so why was he being so cowardly about handling it.

With a deep breath, Billy placed his hands into the straw and wrapped them around the skull. Slowly he pulled it out and started to inspect it. He felt a sudden urge to look into its eyes and when he did do the shed seemed to explode with light. The ground around him began to shake violently and the air was filled with the shriek of aircraft flying overhead and gunfire.

Shocked, Billy dropped the skull and ran out of the shed; slamming the door behind him. As he left the shed, he heard his grandmother's voice calling him from the cottage.

"Time for Tea, Billy!"

He ran back as fast as his legs would carry him, leaving the gate to the orchard open in his haste.

Billy burst into the cottage.

"My word, Billy. That was quick!" His grandmother said peering at him over her half-moon spectacles; her hair drifting in its own wispy way as she wiped her hands on the apron that hung heavy on her; flour-covered from the jam tarts she had been baking that afternoon.

"You look like you've seen a ghost." She laughed.

Billy looked into her sparkling blue eyes and managed a "huh" as he breezed past her through the green tongue and groove wooden door.

"Boots off, Billy!" Gran said pointing at his muddy footwear as Billy started to walk into the room.

Billy stopped and bent down. Quickly he undid his black shabby laces and slipped his boots off. He placed them carefully in the corner of the porch next to an old glazed drain-pipe that held a collection of walking sticks and umbrellas. Now in his stocking feet he headed straight for the kitchen passing the dark unit that stood firm and proud in the sitting room. Checking that his gran wasn't watching he leaped down the three steps that dropped from the sitting room into the kitchen and slid along red tiled floor. Counting back he calculated that he had slid only three sets of tiles. Clearly the scare with the skull had affected him more than he realised as this was nowhere near his record of nine. Gran didn't like this little game he had devised for himself; telling him how he would slip and break something one day whenever she caught him doing it.

Lifting the soles of his feet he inspected the bottom of his socks. They were both a little damp – a sure-fire indication that his boots were leaking – so reducing his ability to slide. With a disapproving grunt he carried on walking over to the kitchen sink.

The green cupboards edging the kitchen reflected the warming glow coming from the roaring fire in the grate.

Billy picked up the bar of soap and began to wash his hands. As he did so all he could think about was the skull he had found in the shed; the main thought being *should he tell his gran?*

Chapter 2

On the Edge of Adventure

Billy dried his hands and sat down at the table. It was covered in a white embroidered table-cloth and there was a big brown teapot in the middle with a matching brown tea-cozy on it keeping the contents warm. Next to it were a home-made loaf of bread and a plate piled so high with home-made jam tarts that Billy thought it reminded him of the tall mountain with crisp snow-capped peaks he had seen pictures of in his favourite book of adventures. Everest he thought it was called.

Billy reached over and lifted the tea-cozy off the teapot and placed it on his head. He loved the warm feel of the cloth, particularly now as his ears were still cold from being outside.

"Make yourself useful and pour the tea then." Gran said as she came down the steps into the kitchen smiling. "I'll dish up the food."

Grinning, with the tea-cozy perched on his head like the headgear of one of those soldiers he had once seen at the changing of the guard at Buckingham Palace, Billy did as requested.

Billy found that he was really hungry and ate his tea quickly. Gran had made his favourite bangers and mash which consisted of two sausages, mashed potatoes and peas–both grown by Gran in her garden. The potatoes were smothered in lashings of thick lumpy gravy. He followed this feast with four jam tarts – two strawberry and two raspberry - to accompany his cup of tea.

"Can I leave the table now please?" Billy asked, wiping his pastry covered fingers on his trousers.

"Of course you can." Gran replied.

Billy noticed that the light was fading outside and the birds had quietened down, readying themselves for the night. A thought burst into Billy's head.

He had dropped the skull on the floor of the garden shed and run. What if he'd left the door open and Ethel or Nancy had wandered in? What if they trampled or sat on it? After all, it was only bone – old bone at that by the look of it – and they were two great big pigs! He should have been less of a scaredy-cat and put it back in the box.

"Gran!" He blurted out loudly almost causing her to choke on the slurp of tea she'd just taken.

"What on earth is the matter?" She said looking worried as she dabbed tea from the corner of her mouth with her handkerchief.

"Can I go check on Ethel and Nancy?" Billy said standing up.

"Whatever for?" Gran said looking mightily confused. "It's dark outside now."

"I… er … think they may be … er …" He said, quickly trying to think of some reason that would seem plausible and not get him into trouble.

He didn't want to own up to having maybe left the garden shed door open. After all, he was supposed to be looking after the old place with his Gran, especially as she was on her own after his grandfather had been posted as missing-in-action during the war.

Billy had moved to live with Granny May when the situation between his parents was not working out. They had told him that it would probably be for the best if they were allowed to have some time together to try and sort out their differences so the decision was made for him.

Granny May lived in the cottage since before the war. Her husband John – Billy's granddad - was reported missing in action not long before the end of the war so when hostilities ceased, she had gone to France in the hope of finding him.

She had never given up hope that he was alive and constantly reminded Billy that if you have nothing else in this life but hope then you have the strength to get through anything. After a fruitless search she had returned to the cottage in England to try and pick up her life again.

"I think they may need some more straw to keep them warm tonight. It looks like there may be a frost." He finally managed to squeeze out.

"Nonsense!" His Gran uttered. "They will be fine. There's plenty of fat on them porkers to keep them warm. Failing that, they'll huddle up together."

Billy's heart sank as he knew not to argue with his Gran.

"Come on." She said. "Help me clear the table. Then you can put another log on the fire and get ready for bed."

Billy helped Granny May stack the dishes by the sink and then made his way to the fire. Reaching down he chose a good solid log from the dwindling pile and placed it on the orange embers in the fire. Sparks and the odd flame danced as the log breathed new life into the fire. There was a warm glow and shadows danced around the dimly lit room; even the shadow of the teapot on the dresser alongside the blue and white china-patterned plates seemed to be dancing.

Once all his chores were done Billy went to his bedroom to get ready for bed. It was a typical boy's room; Meccano strewn on the wood floor boards; a worn wooden-handled catapult hanging off a dark coloured wardrobe handle; a pile of old books on trains and the war. Next to his bed was his favourite illustrated book of adventures.

The front cover of the book had a picture of a sailor and a picture of a bearded mountaineer standing in front of the mountain Billy assumed was Mount Everest. It contained four short stories; one of which was about a climbing expedition up Everest; another about pirates on the high seas; a third about a boy who had built a raft and gotten lost for three days; and his all-time favourite – a war story about D-Day.

Billy quickly slipped into his green-striped pajamas before returning to the kitchen. Standing barefoot on the cold tiled floor, he opened the fridge door and reached in for the glass jug of goat's milk Granny May stored in there. Standing by the sink he poured half a pint into a glass and then returned the jug to the fridge. Carefully he carried his glass over to the kitchen table and set it down; pleased with himself that he had completed the maneuver without spilling a drop. He went over to the cupboard Granny May kept her *treats* in and took out a green biscuit barrel. He lifted its gold lid and retrieved two digestive biscuits. Replacing the lid he returned the biscuit barrel to the cupboard.

Billy sat at the kitchen table with his back to the fire sipping his milk and nibbling on his biscuit. The warming effect of the fire made him feel a little drowsy as he gazed out of one of the two kitchen windows to the rear of the room. As he did so he thought he saw two shadows in the moonlight looming up across the back garden in amongst the pine trees.

"Must have been my imagination" Billy mumbled to himself as he focused on the area in question but saw nothing.

"Did you say something?" Granny May called out from the sitting room next door.

"Oh… er… I was just saying it must be time for bed." Billy quickly answered realising he must have spoken out loud.

"Make sure you brush your teeth before you do." Granny May reminded him.

Billy finished off his milk by washing down the remnants of the second biscuit. He swilled the glass out under the tap and then placed it upside down on the draining board. He went into the sitting room and found Granny May sitting in her favourite rocking chair darning the holes in a pair of his socks while she listened to the radio.

"Good night, Granny." Billy said kissing her on the cheek.

"Good night, my love." Granny replied. "Sleep well."

As Billy walked off to bed down the dimly lit hallway he could just hear the sounds of Elvis playing on the radio. Granny may was softly joining in and Billy smiled. He walked down the hallway and went into the bathroom where he brushed his teeth as ordered and then went into his room. Climbing into bed he suddenly felt sleepy so he switched his light off and settled down for the night. He fell asleep wondering where on earth the skull could have come from.

Chapter 3

Sounds in the Night

RAT-A-TAT-TAT!

Billy woke suddenly to the noise. He looked at his clock and read half past one.

RAT-A-TAT-TAT!

There it was again.

Billy threw back the covers, jumped out of bed and raced to the window. He gazed out over the tin roof that belonged to the old workshop further down the drive. His eyes took a moment to adjust to the darkness, as well as recover from the sleepiness they had been disturbed from, but even then he still couldn't see anything.

Billy listened intently, trying to get a handle on what the noise might have been and where it had emanated from. Recently there had been a fox visiting the cottage and scaring the chickens. Had it been that? Thinking about it he didn't think it sounded very foxlike (though what sound a fox made Billy didn't actually know!) but what else could it have been?

Billy thought long and hard for a moment. Then, Billy had a thought. It was a thought that generated a shiver that ran the length of his spine and made the hairs on the back of his neck prickle.

Could it have been something to do with the skull in the shed?

Billy's imagination was now getting the better of him and running wild. He decided he should investigate so he threw on his thick brown dressing gown. He stood by his door for a moment and listened. The whole house was a still as could be; the quiet only disturbed by the gentle snoring that came from Granny May's bedroom.

He surreptitiously crept out of his room again down the ever familiar hallway.

One, Two, Four.

Billy knew three steps to the left of his bedroom was a creaky floorboard. He'd mastered the trick of avoiding it when he was smaller and had sneaked down to the kitchen for a midnight snack of biscuits and milk.

Billy crept down the passageway. Suddenly, as he passed the kitchen, he had to force himself to hold his mouth shut. A mouse which had been plaguing Granny May shot out from under the table on night time maneuvers in the hope of finding a crumb or two which had fallen from the evening meal. It looked like he'd been lucky too and found something as he was now licking his lips, stopping momentarily to clean his whiskers and mouth before scurrying off behind the dresser.

So that's where his hideaway is Billy thought.

Billy continued his journey.

He managed to make it all the way to the front door without making a sound. Turning the huge old key in the lock he slowly opened the door. He slipped on his boots which were cold against his bare feet and started to walk off down the path. The crazy paving snaked its way around the garden which was well lit by the moonlight.

A thought suddenly occurred to him as Billy remembered that today was actually his birthday. In all the excitement around the discovery of the skull it had completely slipped his mind.

As he left the crazy paving and stepped onto the gravel path the sound of his boots became different. However, Billy was now too engrossed in thinking what Granny May might have got him for his birthday to notice.

He carried on walking around the garden for what seemed like an age – his mind now firmly back on the sound that had drawn him out there – when the gravelly noise from under his feet became silent. He was now walking on the soft pine needles that were strewn like a carpet across the path.

Billy could just make out the silhouette of the pine trees at the back of the cottage where he hoped Granny May was still sound asleep. The moon was giving off a cool glow in the autumn sky – the air crisp and clear – and Billy could see his breath as if it was puffs of smoke billowing from a steam train.

The crunching sound of gravel beneath his feet started again as the pine needles thinned out on the path. Billy stopped dead in his tracks and felt a sudden shiver run down his back. A large, low, lonely shape moved slowly towards him. Billy was frozen to the spot; his heart pounding faster than ever. After all, this was the middle of the night and he was standing there in his dressing gown. The shape came out of the shadows.

Billy was about to let out a yell but which quickly, and fortunately given the quietness of the night, turned into a sigh of relief. The dark figure lumbering towards him was one of the pigs.

"Ethel! You scared me half to death." Billy whispered to the pig. "What are you doing out at this time of the night? And where's that sister of yours?"

A loud rustling from the bushes broke the still of the night air as Nancy came bounding through the shrubbery towards Billy and Ethel. So pleased she was to see him that she bounded into Billy and knocked him over.

"Aaaarrrggghhh, watch it!" Billy called out disgruntled though half aware that someday he would actually find this all funny. "You've gone and got me all mucky now."

Ethel and Nancy both started to snuffle around Billy and prod him with their snouts.

"You two can pack that in as well!" He said, suppressing the need to laugh as their cold snouts tickled his stomach where his dressing gown had fallen open and exposed part of his stomach.

Billy tried desperately to get up off the floor but the two pigs, thinking he was having fun and wanting to play, carried on.

"That's enough, girls!" Billy said as he eventually got up off the floor. "We've got to get you back into the orchard before Granny May hears you."

With that Billy gently herded the two pigs back towards the orchard and through the gate that separated it from the garden; the gate that Billy now realised he'd earlier left open in his haste to get inside the cottage.

Chapter 4

D-Day for Birthday

Billy ushered the two pigs back into the orchard and into their pens. Once he was happy they were secured, and not wanting to make the same mistake again, he closed the gate and double checked the latch.

"Night again, you two!" He whispered.

He decided that he'd had enough excitement for one night and that he would return to the cottage. Besides, there had been no repeat of the noise that had drawn him out there. He was about to start walking back when an owl hooted from the big old oak tree just outside the orchard and then flew straight at Billy. It flew right over him, narrowly missing the top of his head and causing him to duck. He looked up just in time to see it fly over the garden shed, still with its door wide open.

Billy thought about the skull as a cloud wandered over the moon blocking out its light.

He stood there for a moment thinking. Was he brave enough to go into the shed and see if the skull was still there? As if in answer to his question the moon reappeared from behind the cloud and illuminated the shed as if it were a spotlight.

Billy took a big deep breath and walked over to the shed. He hesitated by the open door and then took a tentative step forward. Before he knew it he was standing inside. The skull still lay where he had dropped it. Slowly he walked over to it.

Billy had the weirdest feeling. It felt as if the skull was calling to him to pick it up. He didn't hear voices; it wasn't that sort of calling. It was more of a pulling sensation; like a magnet pulling an iron nail towards it. He decided not to resist and bent down to take the skull in both hands.

Strangely to Billy, the skull felt lighter than he would have imagined. Whenever he'd seen one on the television he always thought they would be solid bone and extremely heavy. The ease with which he lifted it amazed him.

He examined the back of the skull marveling at the smoothness of the bone. It was almost flawless with only a slight crack towards where he imagined it had joined the spine. In a moment of guilt, Billy hoped that the damage had not been a result of him dropping it.

The back of the skull explored, Billy turned it around. The upper jaw was toothless and smack bang in the middle was the gaping nasal cavity. But what drew Billy's attention the most were the eye sockets. They seemed to mesmerise him. Gently he bought the skull up to his face and stared straight into the dark orbital voids.

At first Billy thought there must have been a flash of lightening as the shed seemed to light up. Then he began to wonder if he was actually dreaming. It was, after all, the middle of the night. Then Billy heard a droning noise in the distance accompanied by shouting in both English and what sounded like German (he remembered watching a war film once with sub-titles and the voices shouting sounded very much like that).

BANG!

Billy put his hands to his head as crazily, sand seemed to be blown all over him. He felt something hard and metallic covering his hair. A helmet!

He looked down and found he was no longer wearing his dressing gown. Instead, he was amazed to see he was in uniform! A British soldier's uniform! He was a soldier!!

He looked all around him. Behind him was a vast expanse of water. It was the sea. And peppered across it were row upon row of landing craft with soldiers pouring out of them. Overhead, aircraft droned as they flew in land; the sound of explosions all around him were deafening.

Billy glanced in front of him. Soldiers were streaming up the beach heading for the safety of anything that would give them cover.

All sorts of thoughts ran through Billy's head.

What was going on? All these soldiers pouring out of landing crafts on the beach? Aircraft patrolling the skies? Could it be that he was actually in the middle of…? No that would be crazy surely.

But he remembered seeing an illustration that accompanied one of the stories in his favourite book of adventures that seemed to mirror his new surroundings. And that story was about … D-Day!

"Run for cover, Corp!" A voice shouted out from out of the blue.

Billy felt confused for a moment, not realising the advice was directed at him. Then he glanced across to his right and a soldier was standing there staring at him, urging him on up the beach with his eyes.

"Right you are, mate!" Billy shouted back over the mixture of noises emanating from around him – machine gun fire; soldiers shouting; the throaty roar of mechanical beasts crawling their way up the beach.

He was taken a-back by the deepness of his own voice and when he turned to run over the sand dunes he found it quite easy because he was bigger. The standard issue kit weighed him down a little, not to mention the fact that his boots were soaking wet; presumably from his exit into the sea from the landing craft.

The realisation that he was suddenly an adult hit him full on. Confusion, mixed in with not too little amazement, ran through his mind. How could he be one minute a child standing in his granny's shed holding an old skull and then the next, a full grown soldier on the beaches of one of the most daring, dangerous invasions ever executed in all the years of warfare.

Dangerous! That word seemed to slap Billy in the face. Here he was, in the middle of the beach with who knew how many German battalions bearing down on him with one sole purpose; to riddle him with bullet holes!

Billy quickly glanced back down the sand. The landing craft were falling short of the beach and the soldiers had to jump out into the sea. The German soldiers loved this as it was making the Allied soldiers easy targets. Hundreds of them were falling like flies.

The enemy had positioned a gun, a machine gun, on top of one of the dunes. From there they were able to pepper the beach with bullets. Suddenly, a mortar round landed twenty yards to his left. He was blown off his feet as sand rained down on him yet again. Dazed, he ran his hands all over his body and was relieved to find he hadn't sustained any injuries. Quickly, he got to his feet and ran for the crater that had been created by the explosion. Sitting with his back to the sandy wall, he listened to the cries and moans of the soldiers around him who had fallen; the excitement of the boy he'd been not ten minutes ago wrestling with the philosophical adult he had suddenly become; thinking about how there were so many young men on both side not really wanting to fight but following orders.

Billy shook his head; the soldier in him realising that he couldn't afford to think about it too deeply. When it came down to it, it was him and his men or the enemy.

His men!

Billy realised he must hold responsibility for some of the men. And hadn't the soldier called him Corp? Billy looked down at the sleeve of his tunic. There were the tell-tale stripes.

Blimey! He whispered to himself. *Who'd have thought that!*

This sudden realisation galvanised Billy into action. He knew he needed to re-join the battle and find his men. With a deep breath, he steeled himself and then dived over the top of the crater…

… straight into the wall of boxes in the shed!

For the second time in the last twenty four hours the tower of boxes came crashing down; this time around Billy.

Luckily, Billy was spared a direct hit by any of the boxes and he sat there on the floor of the shed amongst them - his dressing gown now covered in dust and cobwebs – yet still holding the skull in his hands!

Billy stayed still for what seemed like a lifetime – but was probably more like five minutes – hoping that the crash of the boxes would not bring Granny May out of the cottage. When he was sure that he'd got away with it, he stood up.

A slight breeze had built up and the shed rattled a little. It was a rickety old thing at the best of times; the door barely on its hinges; the felt on the roof shredded and torn by the winds and barely hanging on to the boards underneath. Repair work was yet another job on his list of things to do for Granny May.

Feeling confused and wondering what had just happened - mixed in with just a little excitement – he began to restack the boxes again. He located the box that had held the skull and placed it back in; being as careful as possible as he laid it in the straw. Then he searched for a good hiding place for it, choosing to put it behind some old paint cans sitting on the floor to the side of Granny May's wheelbarrow.

He smiled when he saw this as he remembered the hours of fun he and his friends had had taking turns having rides in it around the garden pushed by Granny May.

Billy returned his thoughts to the task in hand.

Thanks to the moonlight shining through the window Billy managed to find some old rags and cloth bags. He covered the paint cans over with them; also concealing the box with the skull. His task complete he exited the shed making sure that this time he had closed the door securely.

He quickly, but quietly, made his way back along the path to the cottage. Carefully opening the door he went back inside, took his boots off and made his way back to bed. He snuggled back under the cover congratulating himself on not waking Granny May.

He lay there for a few minutes looking at the ceiling with thoughts and questions running through his head.

Where had the skull come from? And what had actually happened to him that night? Had he really been on the beach on D-Day and, if so, how on earth had he got there?

With all these questions swirling around his head Billy wondered how he was ever going to get off to sleep. But this last question was soon answered as, with a long yawn, he drifted exhausted off to sleep; his mind on his amazing adventure.

Chapter 5

The Day After The Night Before

The clock read seven a.m. as a bleary eyed Billy woke up to the sound of his gran calling down the hallway.

"Billy Waring? Breakfast!"

This was not the first time she had called him that morning but as she only used his full name when he was in trouble his first thought was one of dread. Had he woken her in the night?

He shot out of bed like a bullet from a gun, his stripy pajama bottoms rolling themselves back down his legs as he bounded down the hallway now filled with rays of sunlight that were breaking through the partly opened bedroom, bathroom and study doors.

Billy rushed through the already open door from the hallway into the sitting room and then on to the kitchen. In front of him was a fully laid breakfast table complete with a small, neatly-wrapped pile of presents waiting for him on his chair. He began to rip them open, not at all carefully. As a family they didn't have a great deal of money and treats were few and far between. So, when it came to birthdays and Christmas, Billy was always a little more than enthusiastic to find out what surprises were hidden beneath the brown paper and garden twine.

Billy thought his face would start hurting from the amount of beaming he was doing as he revealed the presents he had; the usual knitted jumper Granny May had made for him in purple and black this year; a new pair of pajamas; sweets; and his last present, a set of binoculars!

Granny May looked at him and smiled quietly to herself.

"Thanks, Gran!" Billy said as he shot up out of his chair and threw his arms around her almost knocking her cup of tea out of her hand.

"That's alright, lad." She said. "I have one more surprise for you!"

Granny May always had one more present she kept back until the end. She had done this ever since Billy had been living with her. She reached down and pulled a rectangular, well-wrapped gift from under her chair.

Billy had already sat on his chair, now that it was clear of presents. He was cramming a mouthful of tea and toast into his mouth. He was doing a very good impression of a hamster at meal time!

Granny May passed him the parcel.

"Fanks, Gwan!" Billy managed to say in a muffled tone whilst trying not to dribble tea out of his mouth.

The heavy yet flat gift was now being opened at a fast pace. Finally, Billy looked in amazement, his eyes as big as saucers, as he gazed upon the Spitfires, Wellington bombers and an infantryman fully loaded with rifle and bullet-belt running beneath them.

"A World War Two book!" Billy blurted out in excitement. "Thanks, Gran. This might tell me about the sk…"

He suddenly stopped and thought quickly about what he was going to say.

"… er… school in the war."

But Billy thought somehow it was too late. His gran was looking at him with a curious smile on her face.

"Whatever you say, young 'un." She said nodding slowly at Billy and winking in his direction.

Granny May stood up with a knowing look on her face and started to clear the breakfast dishes away.

Chapter 6

A Head for Adventure

Billy was lucky that his ninth birthday was on a Saturday. This meant that after he had fed the chickens and mucked out the pigs his time would be his own. He wasn't bothered so much about the muck they produced but the smell of urine always stuck to the back of his throat. He often thought that the pigs were clever animals having their bed in one corner and their toilet in the other; not like the pet rabbit he used to have that would use the entrance to its bedroom as a toilet and then hop straight through it every time it wanted to run around its pen.

He finished his breakfast and helped Granny May clear the remnants from the table. After thanking his gran once more for his presents he went to get ready to celebrate his birthday; a birthday he didn't know then would possibly be the most exciting birthday of his short life so far.

Back in his bedroom Billy's mind wandered. He thought about his mum and dad who were not with him to celebrate his birthday. Though they had not confided in him about the problems they were having, Billy had been made aware by some of the kids at his old school that his father had done something illegal that made him a criminal. Not being able to live with the shame of whatever he had done his mother and father had decided that they could no longer live in the area. Billy remembered the evening they had called him as he came in from school to talk to him about their problems as if it was only yesterday.

"Come into the living room, Billy." His mother had said. "We have something important we need to discuss with you."

Billy always knew when his mother was troubled. However, this time it felt different. He had nervously walked through the door in his school uniform with his satchel over his shoulder. His father was standing there with his back to the fire. Billy remembered what the boys at school had said and felt angry. For the first time in his life he didn't care if his father shouted at him. Billy hated him for whatever he had done to cause his family to fall apart.

Granny May was there too. She was sat in a straight-backed armchair with her hands resting lightly on its wooden arms.

His father sat down next to his mother on the settee.

"You know we've been having a few problems lately." His mother began. "Well, the three of us have been talking, and Granny May would love for you to go and stay with her at the cottage. You can help her look after the place when you're not at school."

"WHAT ABOUT YOU?" Billy shouted out in disbelief.

"Now calm down, Bill." His father had said.

The tone his father was taking with him made Billy seethe.

"Don't speak to me!" He had screamed at his father. "If it wasn't for you then things would be just fine!"

His father could not have looked more shocked if Billy had gone over to him and slapped his face.

"Your father and me feel we are going to have to move away from here." His mother continued. "I will let you know when we are settled somewhere. Until then, you'll stay with Granny May. One day I will explain to you what it is all about and hopefully you will understand."

Billy turned and run to his room shouting that he would never understand ever. He'd slammed the door and buried his head in his pillow to cry.

Back in his room at Granny May's Billy shook his head and tried to clear his thoughts. He realised that while his mind had been elsewhere in the past he had managed to dress himself. With a tear in his eye he thought about his birthday. They were good and he loved them. But this would be the second one without his mother and the fact that she wasn't there didn't seem to be getting any easier.

The weather was getting colder and Billy had slipped on the new thick jumper Granny May had given him for his birthday. He was wearing his tatty jeans and woolen socks. A quick wash, brush of his teeth and he had sneaked down the hallway. One or two of the doors were still open and a dull light crept through. In the dimness he could just make out the thick-piled wine-coloured carpet and one or two of his grandfather's paintings on the wall; one of the surrounding fields and one of the orchard where Ethel and Nancy now lived with the chickens.

Surreptitiously he left the cottage without as much as a creak from the floorboards or a good-bye kiss from his gran. Granny May understood him and he knew she would be fine with that. The door shut behind him with a dull thud and the latch sat neatly as it dropped into place.

The sun was trying to break through the clouds and the dew was heavy on the lawns. There was a stillness in the air. Even the birds were conspicuous by their absence. Billy liked to watch them weaving and diving around in the sky. He especially liked it when he saw two large black crows dive bombing a bigger than average buzzard. The buzzard knew that it could finish them both off in a split second but chose to just soar higher into the sky then land in a tree some distance away surveying the two avian thugs with interest whilst probably laughing at them.

Did birds laugh? Billy wondered.

The young boy turned his thoughts to the skull.

What was it all about? Had it all been a dream?

He rounded the bend in the path which he had trod only a few hours before. He opened the gate and entered the orchard. He shuffled a few chickens out of his way with his feet.

"Morning, girls." He mumbled as a yawn crept upon him from nowhere.

He headed straight for the shed totally forgetting to feed the puzzled chickens, not to mention the pigs.

Ethel and Nancy turned their attention to the bruised and battered apples on the ground, liking to run their snouts through a combination of mud and autumn leaves. The chickens also decided to seek out an alternative food source, pecking and pulling at anything unfortunate enough to poke its head out of the ground. One large red cockerel, aptly called Red, was having a spot of trouble with a rather fat, stubborn worm. He pulled at it for some time, keeping his head down. Ruffling his feathers he gave one final tug the worm lost the battle and was pulled abruptly from its hole. With one gulp it was gone. Red thrust his head back, shook from side to side and strutted off feeling proud that he had won the prize of another meal.

Billy raised his hand towards the handle on the shed door. With much trepidation in his mind he slowly began to open it. It was stiff as the wood was swollen from the recent rainfall. Billy raised his other hand and grabbed hold of the top of the door. He gently pulled it open, aware that the door could fall off at any moment if he pulled too hard.

Once inside Billy was immediately drawn to the pile of rag-covered paint cans behind which he had hidden the skull the previous night. Sitting on top of them, bold as brass and staring straight back at him was a rat; a big, fat, grey rat! It had a mouth full of straw.

"Gerroff!" Billy shouted at it as he shook his arms in its direction.

The rat scurried off and squeezed through a round hole it had gnawed in the wooden floor boards seeking the safety of the nest it had been making under the shed.

With the rodent out of the way Billy quickly removed the rags from the paint cans and uncovered the box. The rat had gnawed its way through the cardboard and, the opportunity to good to miss, had been helping itself to the straw that had been wrapped protectively around the skull. Billy lifted the box and placed it on the top paint cans. Quickly, he cupped both his hands around out the skull and took it out of the box. It was cold to the touch as he examined it for damage. To his relief he saw no sign of it having been gnawed on by the rat. With a deep breath he brought it up level with his face and stared into its eyes. Billy felt a shiver run straight down his spine and the hairs on the back of his neck stood on end. A bright flash of light lit up the shed and he found himself being flung into a new adventure.

Chapter 7

A Close Shave

Billy was suddenly aware that he was standing in the rain talking to another soldier.

"Of course you can have my bunk for the night." He was saying in his gruff adult voice to a tall, gaunt looking man.

Billy didn't know how but, for some reason, he knew the soldier he was talking to was a dispatch rider who had just ridden into camp on his military motorcycle. It was almost as if all his previous thoughts as a child back at Granny May's had been replaced by the ones that inhabited this new adult body he had invaded. He found that all childish thoughts had disappeared and thinking like an adult came naturally to him; as if it was something he had been doing for a long time.

Billy had been staring into space while he was thinking these amazing thoughts. He came back to reality with a bump and could hear the dispatch rider rattling on about how dangerous his journey had been, unaware that his words were falling on deaf ears.

Billy looked across at the dispatch rider's motorcycle. It was a fine looking beast and he couldn't help smiling to himself as he took in its mechanical beauty. It was dark green in colour with two green boxes; one on either side of the rear wheel. The deep studded tyres were full of mud from the natural terrain and weather conditions the dispatch rider and motorcycle had endured. The dispatch rider noticed the appreciative glint in Billy's eye.

"Some machine, isn't she?" He said with great pride. "Got her back in Nantes. She hasn't missed a single beat all the way down here. I'll almost certainly get one back in Blighty once the wars over. Maybe get me a girl to go with it."

The dispatch rider winked at Billy making him laugh.

"Come on." He said nodding towards the mess tent standing a short distance away to their right; its door flap open enough to let a faint line of light out that illuminated the persistent rain. "Let's get some food into you and then you can tell me all about this machine of yours. I've got a mission to complete later and that machine would be ideal to get the job done."

There was a lack of sound coming out of the tent as the men inside ate in silence.

The dispatch rider frowned and was just about to object to Billy's suggestion that he borrow the motorcycle when there was a loud explosion. At first Billy thought it was thunder. But he soon realised how wrong he was. The Germans had started a covert night raid and it was only by sheer luck that the camp had been missed. He counted the squadron of planes as they flew over; seven German bombers with their distinctive black crosses on their wings rumbled over and disappeared into the distance.

Instinctively, Billy looked back at the camp and ran for his tent. The dispatch rider was close behind him unaware that he was yelling at the top of his voice due to the sound of the exploding bomb having temporarily deafened him. The rain had started to lash down and large puddles were beginning to form all over the camp making it slippery underfoot. Billy stepped right into the middle of one of them.

"Damn it!" He cussed as the water went up his boots. He stood and shook his foot. The dispatch rider stopped by his side.

"I think we'll be ok now." Billy shouted. "Them Jerries must be on a bombing mission somewhere else. Probably got a little trigger happy and dropped us a present when they saw the light down here."

"I'll go and get something to eat then." The dispatch rider shouted back, his ears slowly getting back to normal though he still had an irritating buzz interfering with the sounds around him.

Billy nodded and watched his companion slope off into the mess tent. Happy that the dispatch rider was safely ensconced inside he continued on to his own tent.

Billy turned the flaps back on his tent, walked in and then pulled them back together again to seal out the rain. The faint light from a lamp hanging on a metal hook from the central supporting pole illuminated the sparse interior. The smell of new canvas, a smell he recognised from the shop where he had bought his boots from, filled the tent.

Billy heard another entourage of vehicles pull into the camp. He pulled the flap back a little so that he could peer out and saw the large troop carrier trucks and jeeps coming to a stop in a large parking area to the north of the camp.

This must be some sort of transport division he thought.

Billy could hear the voices of the drivers as they jumped out of their vehicles. He heard them talking about a road being out and that two of the crew had been lost in a night raid. As much as he strained to hear that was all he caught as the drivers disappeared towards the mess tent, their voices muffled by distance.

Billy closed up the tent again and took in his surroundings. In the middle of the tent, secured to the pole from which the lamp hung, was a small mirror. Next to it was a small black iron fire on top of which stood a kettle, alongside which sat a white chipped metallic bowl containing steaming hot water. Above this, hanging from a nail, was a long leather strap curling up at the bottom where it had been pulled up for use. Lying next to it, to Billy's horror, was a large cut-throat razor!

Billy, at the age of nine back in Granny's world, had not had the pleasure of starting to shave as yet. He'd watched his uncle occasionally and marveled at how quickly he would transform his face from a rough sand-papery texture to a smooth, silky finish. However, Billy had only seen his uncle use an electric shaver; never anything as lethal looking as the razor now in front of him. To his horror, he walked over to it and realised that the adult him was preparing to use it to shave!

Billy looked into the mirror and, to his surprise, saw a fair-haired man with a thick bushy moustache staring back at him. His cheeks, with a faint hue of red in them from a combination of the cold rain and warmth from the tent, were covered in stubble. He rubbed his face nervously with his right hand feeling the roughness. With a sigh of resignation he picked up an ivory handled, yellow bristled shaving brush that stood next to the razor.

"Better get on with it then." Billy thought quietly to himself.

He dipped the shaving brush into the bowl and then dabbed it onto a bar of soap conveniently lying next to it. He moved the bristles in a circular motion until he had built up a good lather on it. With a strange confidence he covered his cheeks, enjoying the warmth from the water and the softness of the soap against his skin.

He picked up the razor and ran it along the strap a few times to sharpen it. He stared into the mirror and, noting the determined look in his eyes, began to run the razor upward away from his neck over his stubble.

Billy was amazed at how confidently he had removed the stubble from his face. It was almost like he was an old hand at shaving, not the novice that he knew he was. He rinsed the razor off and then leaned over the bowl to splash water onto his face to remove the last remnants of the soap. As he did so there was a sudden commotion outside in the camp.

Billy quickly dried his face. The noise outside was getting no better and the soldier in him needed to know what was happening. He stepped outside of his tent. It was still raining and water began to drip from his hair. As it ran down his cheeks and off his chin he felt a strange stinging sensation. Billy realised he must have gained a few cuts while performing his first ever shave; first ever in his mind that was though he had the feeling that the adult he was occupying had performed this task a number of times.

The rain was cascading off the tents and small streams were starting to run through the camp. Billy's attention was drawn to the mess tent. He took a couple of steps forward and narrowly missed stepping into one of the streams that was beginning to pick up pace thanks to the torrent of rain that was now eroding the camp floor.

As Billy approached the mess tent he was surprised to see the dispatch rider exit, wearing no shirt. It soon became apparent that he had been arm wrestling the camp chef, Mad Mick, who was undoubtedly the largest soldier in the corp. He stood about six foot one inch tall and always walked with his knuckles facing to the front – a little like a gorilla. His stomach hung over his belt; and his legs and arms, thickly covered in unruly hair, were the size of tree-trunks. Last, but not least, was his trademark beard which occasionally revealed a toothless grin accompanied by a well-furrowed brow.

Billy was again astounded that he knew so much about Mad Mick. How could he know these things without having ever met the man? This all added to the wonder of his new found situation.

Unknown to Billy, it appeared that Mad Mick, in his gruff booming voice, had started calling the dispatch rider a *Pretty Boy* which, obviously, the dispatch rider took exception to. Fuelled up on beer he decided to challenge Mad Mick, the strongest man in camp, to an arm wrestling competition.

They had sat down at the nearest table and without as much as another word they locked hands. Before the dispatch rider knew what was happening Mad Mick wrenched his opponents arm down to the table. There was a loud crack as the table collapsed and in an instant the dispatch rider was prostrate on the floor. He pushed himself up; his face contorted in pain as he nursed a now dislocated shoulder.

"Think yourself lucky, Pretty Boy." Mad Mick growled. "You've still got one good arm left to tie your boot laces with. Next time you challenge me you'll be having to use your teeth to do them up!"

Mad Mick turned to walk through the crowd which had quickly formed to watch the spectacle. Battle over, they scattered to both sides and dispersed as quickly as they'd gathered.

Not aware of the dispatch rider's challenge and misfortune, Billy assumed that the man staggering out of the mess tent was drunk. It was only when he mumbled something about Mad Mick and arm-wrestling before falling flat on his face in the mud that Billy realised that the dispatch rider was shirtless not in celebration but because he was using it as a crude sling to support his injured shoulder.

Billy walked over to the dispatch rider and bent down. He slid his arm through the cold, wet mud until it was fully under the stricken man's armpit. He dragged him up and then pulled him through the camp back towards his tent.

"What the hell happened?" The dispatch rider groaned as Billy dragged him through the flaps of the tent and lowered him on the bunk.

Billy went around to the head of the bed and raised the dispatch rider to a sitting position. He straddled his legs across the bed and then settled himself behind the injured man. Looping his right arm around the dispatch rider's problematic shoulder Billy took a deep breath.

"Right, mate." He whispered into the ear of the agonised man in front of him. "Unfortunately this is going to hurt like the blazes."

The dispatch rider turned and looked a Billy, a puzzled look on his face. Then he realised what Billy was about to do. Fear flowed across his face and he started to struggle but Billy had a firm grip on him.

"Won't take long." Billy said through gritted teeth and with an almighty tug on the dispatch rider's shoulder Billy popped it back into place.

The pain was too much for the stricken man and after letting out an ear piercing scream, he passed out.

Billy stood up and then lay the dispatch rider's head down on the bed. He was out cold.

Probably the best place for him Billy thought knowing that when he did wake the dispatch rider would be in excruciating pain.

Billy threw a standard issue, itchy green blanket over the battered soldier and decided it was time to think about leaving on his mission. With the dispatch rider incapacitated he was in no position to object to Billy borrowing his motorcycle.

After collecting his kit bag and donning his wet gear the tall blonde man Billy occupied and who still held so much mystery to him was ready to go. He was just about to leave the tent when, all of a sudden, a rather large pink pig flashed in front of his eyes!

Confused, Billy walked out of the tent and across to the motorcycle. The machine was wetter than ever but still looked amazing; the reflection of the camp gas lamps flickering on the iron horse.

Billy wiped the seat with his hand and sat astride it. He flicked the stand up and, felt the machine wobble in his hands. He placed his right foot on the kick-start and, standing tall, dropped all his weight onto it. The motorcycle fired into life and Billy revved the motor to keep it going. Giving the engine time to warm up Billy strapped his kit bag to the back of his seat. He sat back and revved the motor some more; just as another image of a pig ran across his vision. With a flash of light he was back inside Granny May's old shed. The skull had slipped from his hands and there, nudging him, was Nancy!

Chapter 8

Nearly Caught

"What were you thinking, you stupid pig!" Billy yelled out in Nancy's direction. ""That was turning into one of the best adventures I've ever had."

He was now sitting on the floor to the shed.

If ever a pig could look sorry then Nancy was doing just that. She hung her head low and slowly backed out of the shed, nearly taking an old sack and half the tools with her.

"Guess I'll have to go somewhere and lock the door next time I pick up the skull with my bare hands." Billy said quietly to himself.

He picked himself up off the floor and dusted himself down. Then he heard Granny May's angelic voice approaching the orchard. She was singing a song she had heard on the radio. Granny May did like to sing.

Billy thought it was a good job that he'd returned when he did because he didn't know how he would explain to Granny May what had happened to him. Maybe the pesky pig had done him a favour after all.

Granny May approached the gate. She couldn't see Billy anywhere.

"Billy!" she cried out sounding a little angry.

Where is that boy? She was thinking.

Billy heard the annoyance in Granny May's voice and knew he was in trouble. In truth, he thought he would much prefer to go and face an army of German soldiers than his Granny May. After all, having completed his chores, he had no legitimate reason to be in the shed.

Billy quickly thought as Granny May came through the gate.

"I'm in the shed!" He yelled before engaging his brain and letting Granny May know where he was. "Those blasted pigs!"

"What have I told you about using language like that?" Granny May called back. "Next time I'll wash your mouth out with soap and water like I did your cousin Archie for saying Molly Atkins had a face like a baboon's bottom!"

Billy sniggered just as he had done the first time he heard Archie say it. Molly Atkins was improving with age. She hadn't got such a baboon's ass for a face anymore. In fact, Billy secretly had feelings for her that he didn't quite understand as yet.

"Well, boy!" Granny May continued. "What have the pigs got to do with you being in the shed?"

As her head appeared at the door Billy could see that her eyes were scanning the shed for vital clues as to what he was really doing in there.

"They must have pushed against the door and dislodged it." Billy said quickly. "Nancy was rooting around in here."

Just as he said this he looked to his left and was horrified to see the skull peering out from underneath the wooden workbench; another of his grandfather's creations.

"Shall we go outside?" Billy said as he ushered his granny out of the shed.

Billy was just about to shut the door behind him when Granny May grabbed his arm.

"Wait!" She said. "Don't shut that just yet."

Billy's heart missed a beat and then sank.

"You can add that to your list of chores for the day." Granny May continued. "I'm off to town for some shopping and business I need to attend to. Make sure those leaves and door are both dealt with."

Billy nodded eagerly despite being given these additional tasks to do..

"See you later, alligator!" Granny May said half smiling.

"In a while, crocodile!" Billy gave the expected reply.

Granny May had used the saying ever since Billy was a toddler and he figured it was her way of saying she was the matriarch in their relationship and he would do well to remember he was still a young boy. Billy played along just to humour her. After all, he loved her and did actually enjoy living with her.

By the time Granny May arrived home from her expedition the leaves had been raked up and Billy had got a good smoky fire going. He had also fixed the shed door after remembering to put the skull back in the box and re-covering it with the rags; relieved that he had recovered from the heart stopping moment when he thought Granny May had seen the skull.

Chapter 9

Hide and Skull

Billy was excited because his cousin Arthur was about to visit with his Auntie Eve and Uncle Sid.

Granny May had got her best pinafore on and, as was usual whenever they had guests to stay, had made up the spare room. Billy had fixed the old brown headboard back on the bed and moved a few boxes out into the library. He had dusted the cobwebs off the light which Granny May could not reach. He thought he must have looked funny standing there on a chair with a feather duster! He was only glad she hadn't made him wear her pinafore too!!

The gravel driveway was about a hundred yards long. It ran alongside an old wood and had a metal fence dividing the two. Bracken and brambles grew through the old rusty rails. Tufts of grass had started to break through the driveway and the potholes were still full of water after a good April downpour.

Billy came out of the veranda door; a rickety old sliding door with a homemade handle his grandfather had carved in his workshop. A car was coming up the driveway. Billy knew it was his aunt and uncle. The car window must have been open as the rabble – his nickname for them – were being just that.

"It's not fair!" He heard the yell of Cousin Arthur. "Billy's got all this to play in!"

"Yes. And you've got it for the whole weekend too." Said Auntie Eve.

"Enough of that nonsense!" Uncle Sid shouted out in his usual old grumpy tone.

Billy smiled quietly to himself as the car, a black Morris Oxford, came into view from around the privet hedge that surrounded the orchard and animal enclosure. It came to a crunching stop outside the cottage.

"Billy!" They shouted as they all clambered out of the car.

"Hello, Uncle Sid. Auntie Eve." Billy replied as they gave him a big hug.

His cousin Arthur, or Archie as he liked to be called, hung back then joined Billy smiling.

"Hi, Cuz." He said.

"Hi, Archie." Billy replied. "Have we got some adventures to have this week-end!"

"Enough time for adventures later." Uncle Sid said. "You two boys can help bring the luggage in."

With that, he grabbed Auntie Eve's hand and marched up the veranda.

"Where's that mother of mine?" He shouted out. "Baking and dusting; polishing and fussing, no doubt!"

Granny May had just taken off her pinafore and left it in the kitchen, neatly folded. She rushed up the steps through to the sitting room, quickly adjusting her hair in the mirror. She emerged through the veranda door her face beaming.

"She's here!" She said.

It had been three long years since they had last seen each other. After hugs and kisses they were all soon sitting around the table with half-drunk cups of tea in front of them and biscuit crumbs down the front of their cardigans and shirts.

The boys had put the luggage in the rooms; two dirty old brown suitcases in Auntie and Uncle's room and a green ruck sack in Billy's room which he would be sharing with Archie.

Auntie Eve, Uncle Sid and Granny May were totally unaware that the two boys had slipped out to play hide and seek.

Billy and Archie, hands in their pockets, trudged down the path. They both kicked stones as they rounded a bend in the path by the delphiniums. Billy thought they looked like rockets racing up to the sky.

"Here's a great place to start." Archie said.

There was an old concrete toadstool covered in moss at the side of the path. Billy and Archie agreed to toss a coin to see who would hide first and who would be the seeker. Billy took a shilling out of his pocket. It had belonged to his grandfather and was a treasured possession.

"Heads." Archie correctly chose.

"You hide first then." Billy said closing his eyes and beginning to count.

"1,2,3,4…10..15..30..35..40.." He counted up to a hundred. "Ready or not, here I come!"

Whilst Billy was counting Archie had run up the steps next to the stone toadstool and headed off right under the pine trees towards the old wood shed and then doubled back towards the orchard to try and confuse Billy. He kicked an old apple which hit the tool shed and bounced back at him.

"I heard that!" Billy called out as he ran up the steps to the lawn.

Archie flung open the wooden door, ripped back the sheet covering the paint cans, sat down and covered himself up. His breathing became low as he tried to conceal himself further. He could hear Billy as he neared the shed. The shed door continued to flap in the breeze almost as if to draw Billy's attention to Archie's hiding place.

It was now around five o'clock and the light was beginning to fade. Billy looked back through the shrubs and the pine trees.

Soldiers standing to attention Granny May told him that his grandfather had called them. In fact, he'd named the tallest one The General.

The shed door gave one final bang startling Billy.

He crept along the orchard dodging the fallen apples that carpeted the floor, reached up to pull the shed door open and ... *bang* … the door slammed again. He heard a loud thud and then the clatter of cans as they rolled from the neat stack that had sat there for a number of years.

Billy had never understood why Granny May had held on to so many old, half empty tins of paint as he could not remember her ever using, or asking him to use, them for any paint jobs around the place.

"Billy!" Archie yelled.

Billy flung the door open and, to his amazement, saw Archie lying on his back, his legs up against the opposite wall and his head still covered by the sheet.

"Billy!" He shouted again.

Billy could detect an uneasiness about Archie's voice. Fearing his cousin was hurt he quickly pulled the sheet off him. A look of amazement crept over his face and he had a rush of excitement. Archie looked at Billy's face.

"Go on, tell me the worst!" Archie whimpered. "My head's fallen off, hasn't it!"

"Don't be daft!" Billy laughed.

Archie pulled himself round and put his hands towards what he thought was a head shaped log. The light was fading faster now especially in the shed. Billy knew what it was and it wasn't a log or Archie's head. It was the skull!

"That's my skull!" He said without thinking and lunging forward to pick it up.

"Now who's being daft?" Archie said still dazed by the speed of the previous events. "Your head's not dropped off either!"

Billy looked into the skulls eyes. There was a bright flash and Billy was transported out of the shed!

Chapter 10

Under a Jerry Sky

Billy found himself running up a path. It twisted and turned and the stones under his feet crunched. The light seemed to be fading in this world too but Billy could just make out the dry-stone wall to his left. Gorse bushes overhung it and moss was beginning to cloak the stonework.

Off to his left there was a grass bank and then more gorse bushes leading to scrubland. In the distance Billy could see sand dunes undulating their way across the horizon like the humped backs of dinosaurs ready to reveal themselves to the world.

As Billy continued running the path became a little steeper. The wall began to slowly reduce in height until his head was almost level with it. Gradually his head, then his shoulders, appeared above it until he was able to see what lay past it.

The gorse was thinning out and beyond it he could see white houses – some still with their laundry hanging out; others their lines broken and hanging by a thread to the poles so that the washing was dragging on the floor.

To the right of one of the houses, Billy could make out a pile of rubble. He was just about to jump onto the wall to investigate when, all of a sudden, there was an almighty bang! It was louder than any firework Billy had ever heard. To his amazement, he just caught a glimpse of the barrel of a gun protruding through what used to be a window. A German tank had parked itself inside the house which it was cleverly using for camouflage.

It fired another shot that sailed over Billy's head just missing him and exploding in the scrubland. Billy crouched back down below the wall. He decided in a split second to do what seemed natural in a situation like this. He crawled back to where he could stand so that the wall protected him fully and, despite being burdened by his heavy back pack and gun, stood up and ran like the wind! Billy had heard of an athlete called Jesse Owens that could run really fast but he was sure this particular corporal could have given him a run for his money, especially with a tank firing at him! In a moment of humour Billy thought that this could be an interesting way of getting some of the slower runners in the Olympics to pick up their pace!

Billy ran down the hill along the craggy stone path with surprising ease. Pine trees had started to spring up on both sides and the stone wall that had protected Billy had now disappeared. The woodland grew thicker and the light was diminishing as the night began to draw a veil over the daylight.

Billy heard what he thought was an owl in the distance. Then he could just make out the faint dulcet tones of a voice calling out.

"Corp! Corp!"

Billy rounded a bend in the path almost sliding on the loose stones underfoot. In front of him he could see one solitary flashlight.

"Run, Corp!" A second voice called out through the darkness.

The crunching sound of gravel disappeared and he could now hear wood underfoot as his heavy boots propelled him forward. The surface beneath him began to sway gently from side to side as if he were on a boat. But Billy knew this wasn't so. He was actually on a bridge.

"Jump, Corp! Jump!!"

Billy heard the voice close by. As he leapt forward a shell from the tank exploded under the bridge leaving him hanging in mid-air.

Then something peculiar began to happen.

"Corp…Corp... Billy… Billy…"

Chapter 11

A Tale To Tell

Billy, dazed and confused, at first wondered what was going on. How had his cousin, Archie, entered this dangerously exciting world he had discovered?

"Billy? Are you alright? What was going on? Who's Jesse Owens?" Archie was bombarding him with questions.

Billy realised that he must still be in the tool shed. But where was the wooden floor underneath his feet or the cold draft that blew through the holes in the door?

His eyes began to focus a little better. There was a faint light and the smell of Granny May's cooking. He opened them wide which made him look like a startled animal, probably one of those possums from Australia he'd heard about.

"What ...? Who ...? Where ...?" Billy began.

"Me first!" Archie said. "Where ..? Who ...? What was going on?"

Billy sat upright in bed.

"The skull!" He said without thinking.

"It's alright, Billy. I've hidden it behind the old tools in the corner of the shed. I couldn't wake you up."

"What do you mean?" Billy said, his head still feeling fuzzy.

"Well I couldn't wake you up." Archie explained. "So I ran through the garden, down the steps and in through the back door to the kitchen. I told Granny May what had happened and Dad heard and came running to help you."

Billy looked startled.

"You ... you didn't mention the skull did you?" He asked nervously.

"I did …" Archie began then paused for dramatic effect taking in Billy's horrified face. "… not!"

After the relieved laughter had died down Archie turned and walked out of the room.

"Come on." He said. "It's suppertime. Granny May says you can come and have something to eat if you're feeling up to it"

"Try stopping me!" Billy said throwing the heavy quilt and blanket off the bed.

He swung his legs around and hopped onto the floor. He pulled his brown dressing gown off the back of the door and threw it on. He tied the brown and white rope chord that acted as a belt around his waist. The wool of the dressing gown kept him nice and warm but it always made him itch where it came into contact with his skin. Billy slipped his fingers under the collar and scratched his neck.

As he made his way down the hall towards the front room a thought about his new found adventures niggled in his mind.

What if he managed to get stuck in the other time?

He had not experienced this loss of time before and it made him doubt whether he should risk picking the skull up ever again. Billy tried to put these thoughts out of his mind. He walked into the front room and found the table adorned with a multitude of pastry treats.

"How's my favourite nephew doing?" Uncle Sid boomed across the room.

This was one of his uncle's favourite, and repetitive, sayings on account of the fact that Billy was his only nephew. "Quite a bang on the head that must have been."

Billy was just about to ask what bang on the head Uncle Sid was referring to when he caught sight of Archie's face. He was staring intently at Billy with a very nervous look and furrowed brow. Realising that Archie must have told Uncle Sid, Auntie Eve and Granny May some story to cover for why Billy had been how he was, he nodded back in his cousin's direction.

"Yes, it must have been." He said slowly, rubbing his head for dramatic effect.

Auntie Eve and Granny May came swiftly into the room and flung their arms around him.

"You had us worried there for a moment." Granny May said fluffing around him.

"But you're alright now, aren't you?" Auntie Eve asked.

"He's ok." Uncle Sid said to them both trying to reassure them. He's always in the wars, aren't you, Billy?"

*More than you kno*w! Billy thought and couldn't help laughing.

"I'm fine. Really." Billy said extricating himself from Auntie Eve's smothering hugs.

Granny May gave him an inquisitive look that made Billy feel that she knew exactly what had been going on. Unknown to Billy, Granny May was well aware of the skull and already making plans to move it from the tool shed.

"That's good then." Auntie Eve decreed. "Now, supper then bed boys."

After eating enough food and drinking enough milk to keep an army marching for days Billy and Archie were soon washing their faces, brushing their teeth and then jumping into bed.

"Night, Billy." Archie called out sounding excited. "I can't wait until tomorrow."

"Night, Archie" Billy replied and fell fast asleep.

Chapter 12

Archie's Story

The next day Archie found himself with time to kill on his own. Granny May had tasked Billy with his daily chores and told him that he could "mess about" with his cousin as soon as he had finished them. Archie decided to use the time to explore the orchard and see what the two pigs were up to. As he did so he was drawn to the toolshed.

The young lad mad his way up to the rickety building and, with a quick glance around him to make sure no-one was watching, pulled the door open and stepped in. Once safely inside he secured the door behind him.

He approached the pile of paint tins hiding the skull with a little trepidation. Taking a deep breath, he removed the sheet and reached down to retrieve the box; closing his eyes and hoping that he didn't feel anything run across his hand. His bravery could only withstand so much and he knew that should there be the slightest hint of a mouse, or even worse, one of those fat juicy-bodied spiders coming into contact with his skin he would end up rapidly leaving the shed; probably screaming like a girl.

To his relief, no such trauma befell him.

He lifted the box and placed it carefully on the top paint tin. He peeled back the lid and stared intently at the skull within. Before he could lose his courage he grasped it with both hands and lifted it free of the straw. Almost at once he found himself staring into its dark, lifeless eye-sockets.

Archie felt light-headed and giddy. With a sensation like the falling feeling he got when he was dreaming he was transported into another world.

Archie couldn't believe what had happened to him. One minute he had been in Granny May's shed; the next he was alone in a tunnel! The darkness he had emerged into gave Archie the shivers and the slightest noise was magnified to appear much louder than it was. He was suddenly aware that he could hear something.

At first Archie thought the noise was the steady drip of water through the stone ceiling but he soon realised it wasn't that. The sound he could hear was the muffled echoes of voices bouncing off the stone walls and arched ceiling above him. He froze to the spot for a second then noticed an alcove. He could just make out a flickering light coming towards him as he slipped through the gap in the wall. Holding his breath, he waited and watched as two German soldiers passed by him, unaware of his presence.

The air in the tunnel was cold and Archie was careful not to let his breath out immediately. When he did, he was careful not to release it too quickly in case the sound of it gave him away. The two soldiers walked further away; their voices becoming quieter by the second until they filed out of sight.

Archie was not happy about the unbelievable predicament he had found himself in. Suddenly, he found the feet beneath him start moving quickly forward with purpose. He desperately tried to slow the quickening pace but to no avail. He did not seem to be in control of them and it seemed there was nothing he could do but go along for the ride.

It was then that Archie became aware of something tickling his nose. Thinking he may have actually realised his worst nightmare and become attached to a spider he reached up to swipe it away. To his surprise he discovered hair on his top lip.

At that moment there was a slight break in the roof of the tunnel and a faint shaft of sunlight was forcing its way through the darkness. As he passed through it, Archie had time to see that he was no longer in the clothes he had been wearing at Granny May's but was in full army combat uniform. To say he was confused would be an understatement. But he didn't have chance to analyse what was going on as, in his haste, he managed to kick a loose stone across the floor of the tunnel. The sound of it ricocheting off the surrounding rock was amplified by the tunnel and echoes seemed to resonate around him.

Archie had no time to react or no way of knowing what was to happen next.

"Halt!" A heavily accented voice shouted out of the dark in anger.

Suddenly there was a flash followed by the sharp sound of a shot being taken. Archie felt a sudden pain in his left hand and fell to the ground. He tried desperately to crawl away from the direction of the shot but was hindered by the pain running down his left arm every time he moved. Then he felt a short, sharp kick on the sole of his foot. He turned onto his back and looked up; straight into the barrel of a German rifle. He had never felt so scared in his life and was convinced he was about to die.

Out of the dark two hands grabbed him by the scruff of his jacket and hauled him to his feet. The darkness around him seemed to swirl and Archie thought he was going to pass out. He closed his eyes for a second and preyed.

When Archie re-opened them he was back in the toolshed.

"What on earth do you think you're doing in here!?" Billy cried out.

"I … I … just wanted …" Archie tried to get out but couldn't.

Billy stood there shaking his head.

"I turn my back for one minute and …" He began and then, seeing how shook up Archie was, softened his voice. "You've come a right cropper against the lawn roller. How's your hand?"

Billy pointed at Archie's left hand. His cousin examined his injury and winced as the pain suddenly grew in intensity.

"You've been on an adventure." Billy said looking excited. "What happened?"

"I don't want to talk about it." Archie replied indignantly. "And as for me joining the army? Not bloomin' likely!"

With that last statement Archie turned and marched out the toolshed, still clutching his injured arm. Billy stared after him bemused and then, with a sigh of resignation, began to tidy the toolshed again.

Chapter 13

The Fields Below

Billy's mind switched back to his own mission. He had gone awhile now without handling the skull, what with trying to keep his cousin Archie entertained and all the chores Granny May kept throwing at him. He sometimes imagined her as a drill instructor in one of his adventures.

His adventures! He had not had one for a few days now and it was beginning to show. He had become snappy and grumpy with people. Even Granny May was getting concerned. Still he would be fine after another adventure.

Without hesitation Billy picked up the skull and stared into its eye sockets. With a flash of the now familiar light he was transported to his other world!

Billy emerged into his new adventure feeling quite strange. He felt a little disorientated. It was like when you are away and wake up in a strange room and it takes you a moment to work out where you are.

It took him a few seconds to get his bearings. Initially he thought that he was enveloped in fog. But then realisation set in and he began to let out the world's longest, though silent, scream. It wasn't fog. It was clouds! And he was hanging there, in mid-air, amongst them on the end of a parachute.

He kicked his legs in blind panic until the adult he had become suddenly began to take over. A strange calmness fell over him and all of a sudden the situation felt like second nature to him. With a huge sigh he relaxed and waited with baited breath for what looked like was going to be another exciting adventure

*

As he floated there in the sky he suddenly felt something whizz past his head and ricochet of his helmet.

A bullet!

Billy looked up and was relieved to see that the deflection from his helmet had averted a disastrous encounter between the bullet and his parachute canvas. It was unscathed and still fully inflated allowing him to continue gently gliding towards the ground.

Billy realised he had been subconsciously gripping onto the webbing securing him to the parachute for grim death so relaxed his grip a little. As he stared down and focused on the scene unfolding below he could just make out what appeared to be a small town. The lights flickered even though daylight was beginning to slowly break through the night sky.

More gun fire rattled through the air and Billy could now hear voices.

German voices!

The hairs stood up on the nape of his neck and something caught his attention.

He had a rifle hanging across his chest.

A small wave of fear washed over Billy. How on earth would he land safely? Then he thought logically and remembered that this wasn't actually him. He was again in the body of the same soldier from previous adventures. The same soldier that presumably the skull belonged to.

Billy felt calm again. Obviously the soldier had been trained for missions like this. All Billy had to do was go along for the ride. With this in mind he instinctively looked around him. To his left and right the sky was filled with parachutes; some with soldiers hanging there gripping their guns as he was; others, lifeless. Billy saw at least one soldier praying vigorously to his God. Billy found comfort in the fact that he was not on his own as more troops cascaded out of the planes above the sea of canvas surrounding him.

Billy didn't know what part of the war this was but he knew he had to prepare for his landing on a windswept field on the edge of the town. The ground crept up on him quickly and the houses below were getting bigger. He could hear more voices intermingled with the sound of vehicles.

He grabbed hold of his rifle in both hands; one on the stock while he placed his finger over the trigger. He hit the ground quite hard and instinctively rolled over - how he had been taught, he presumed. His parachute, slightly torn at the edge and blowing in the wind, worked its way across the field dragging Billy behind it. Without a second thought he released the webbing and freed himself. Slowly he opened his eyes and focused on the scene around him.

Birds sang whilst they flew overhead, dodging the manufactured beasts of the air as they swooped amongst them. There was a faint smell of wild flowers on the breeze and Billy's mind quickly raced back to the long hot summer days at his Gran's.

The birds broke Billy's thoughts as the singing turned into short bursts of chattering. As the young soldier began to pick his head up he heard someone shout.

Billy should not have landed in this field. The wind had blown him off course. He was lucky he hadn't been blown in the opposite direction as he could have been stuck on the steeple of the town's church or, as he had sometimes heard tales of, been battered by a vicious elderly lady with a rolling pin defending herself from the invading Allies. He had often wondered if this was one of those myths that got bandied around but he was grateful he wouldn't have to find out. Besides, why would such an old lady do such a thing if the Allies were there to liberate her town?

Billy's soldier shook his head to clear his mind of such trivial thoughts. He needed to think about his mission and how he was to survive it.

Billy had lost his regiment by drifting off course. The rest had moved off deeper inland to defend to win back territory from the enemy and then defend it until reinforcements arrived.

Feeling exposed on his own, Billy looked around for somewhere to take cover. He noticed that there was a small copse of trees on the edge of the field and decided to make his way quickly over to it. Concentrating hard on his sanctuary he failed to see a rock protruding from the ground and tripped over it. As he fell he let go of his rifle so that he could break his fall and suddenly found himself back in Granny May's toolshed. By dropping the rifle in one world, he had simultaneously dropped the skull in the other so bringing his latest adventure to an abrupt end.

Chapter 14

The Rite of Passage

Billy felt a bit disgruntled at being rudely torn from such an exciting adventure so he quickly picked the skull back up, hoping to re-join it as the soldier raced across the exposed field. However, he was soon in for a surprise as he was propelled into a completely different adventure; one that he was no longer alone in.

Billy found himself running through a forest alongside another soldier. Suddenly they came to a stop and the two breathless soldiers leant on each other for a few minutes.

"Shook … em … off … then?" Billy's comrade managed to piece the sentence together in between sharp breaths in the cool night air.

"Looks like you might … be right … old chap." Billy managed a longer but still laboured answer

They both listened intently for the faintest noise: a twig snapping under the boot of an enemy soldier or even a whisper in German. They came to a decision quickly.

"Nothing!" They said together and then laughed at their simultaneous announcement.

It was the thick set Goliath of a man who slumped down first on the all too familiar wet ground. On this occasion, the sound was different.

"Do that again!" Billy urgently instructed.

Billy's comrade looked up at the steely faced soldier peering down at him and snorted.

"You do it. I've been waiting for this sit down for hours!"

Billy raised his boot off the ground and thrust it back down between the goliath's knees with all the force he could muster.

"Hey, watch it!" The sitting man cried out in alarm. "That could've been painful!!"

"Listen!" Billy said to his comrade sounding insistent as he raised his boot again giving plenty of warning this time before he brought it crashing down again.

This time Goliath heard it. A hollow, wooden sound emanated from beneath Billy's boot and vibrated Goliath's backside where he sat.

"What the …" He exclaimed as he scrambled backwards before standing up.

Curiosity had given him a new lease of life and the fatigue that had floored him moments before was temporarily forgotten. Billy was already brushing the dead leaves from the patch where Goliath had previously been sitting. Goliath joined him.

With enthusiasm, the two comrades frantically scraped yet more autumn debris from the ground, stopping occasionally to see if they could hear anything looming towards them through the night. Before long they had cleared some of the area and had revealed wooden boards.

Billy scrambled around the area in front of him. As he did so he felt something metallic in the grass. He cleared the soil from around it and revealed what appeared to be a hooped handle. With one hand he gently pulled at it.

"What you doing?" Goliath called out. "There could be anything down there!"

"I kind of figured that bit out already." Billy replied with a hint of sarcasm. "Those leaves were well caked to the wood. I'd hazard a guess that these doors haven't been opened in a good while."

Goliath pondered this for a second before agreeing.

"Besides," Billy continued, "if that is the case, anything that went down there ain't coming out alive."

Goliath nodded and leaned down to grasp the metal loop. Both men pulled and the door flew open with a scream of rusty hinges. The noise reverberated around the wood.

They glanced nervously about them and strained their ears to listen.

Nothing.

They both peered into the hole and saw a set of wooden steps leading down into the ground. Goliath, on account of being the biggest, reversed onto the steps and descended to the floor below; closely followed by Billy.

Billy very quickly deduced from the smell of dampness, the lack of noise and the absence of any air movement that he was in some sort of underground bunker. Goliath's voice broke his concentration.

"There's boxes down here, mate!" He called out

Before him, a Goliath was lifting a lid as he spoke.

Billy found himself rummaging around in the dark.

"Bottles!" Goliath suddenly exclaimed as he and grabbed hold of two elongated items and rattled them together. He reached down and pulled out another bottle from the crate. As his eyes grew accustomed to the darkness he thought he could just make out a cork sticking out of the neck of the bottle.

"Well, what is it?" Billy said impatiently.

"Give a man a chance!" Goliath fired back and then proceeded to pull the cork out of the bottle with his teeth and spat it on the floor next to him.

He raised the bottle to his nose and took a deep breath. His eyes lit up.

"Cognac!" He announced and put the neck of the bottle to his lips.

Goliath managed to gulp down half the contents of the bottle without pausing for breath. Billy found himself reaching for the bottle.

"Hey, save some for me, you animal!"

"Plenty more where that came from I should guess!" Goliath said and then let out a large belch.

Billy took his cue and reached down into the box for a bottle of his own.

The two soldiers made the most of their new found treasure and when they woke the following morning felt the after effects of their alcohol fuelled evening.

Billy came around in the toolshed where he was sat next to the skull nursing a sore head. He staggered to his feet and weaved his way back to his room, fortunately managing to avoid Granny May and the rest of the family. He felt very tired and very giddy so, despite it being early afternoon, went straight to bed.

When he rose out of bed later that day, Granny May having woken him by shouting him for his tea, his head throbbed. He thought back to his adventure and wondered, could he be suffering a hangover? He'd seen his father, and even Uncle Sid, in a few states before brought on by drinking so he suspected it was. That being so, he decided there and then that it wasn't a good feeling and he would be very wary of how much he drank when he grew up!

As they ate their tea, Billy and Archie sat in an uncharacteristic silence. Normally they would be told to be quiet at the table but tonight they didn't seem to have much to say. Occasionally they would glance at each other, each aware that they had had some sort of adventure that had not exactly been pleasant though not knowing, or wanting to share, the details of those adventures.

Having completed their evening chores, and to the astonishment of Granny May, Uncle Sid and Auntie Eve, they said goodnight and turned in early. Before long they were fast asleep, recuperating from the exertions of their adventures.

Chapter 15

Granny May's Secret

May gently opened the bedroom door and made sure the two boys were settled down for the night after their ordeal in the shed. Satisfied that they were fast asleep she quietly closed it again.

"Night my little soldiers." She whispered smiling as she did so.

It was now fully dark outside and May had decided she should use this darkness to go out to the garden shed, recover the skull and relocate it. The events of the night had shaken everyone but May was pleased that the suspicions she had held over the last year or so had finally been confirmed. The skull had been discovered!

With mixed feelings of joy and horror she was glad that the right person – well, the right person in her eyes anyway – had discovered the secret. A secret she had managed to hide under a veil of deceit for all these years since her return from France.

She walked down the long narrow hall and into the front room where, at last, the only other people that knew of the skulls existence would now spend time picking over the consequences of the re-awakening of old memories.

Sid and Eve had been tidying away the plates and cutlery from tea time. May's food was legendary not to mention Eve's own ability to feed the masses on bare essentials. After all, rationing was still in place and had taught her to be imaginative with her culinary skills.

Sid looked up at May and smiled. Eve was just coming out of the kitchen and headed straight towards May who was now nearing her favourite chair. Eve smiled and flung her arms around a very tired looking May, giving her a very enthusiastic hug.

"You alright, old girl?" Eve asked looking concerned.

"Will be when I've finished." May replied looking straight into her daughter-in-law's emerald eyes. "It was inevitable, I suppose, that this would happen. That boy's got more of his Granddad John in him than he knows. He's even mentioned joining up. Going into the forces."

"Funny that, eh Eve?" Sid chirped up. "The two scoundrels must have been scheming something up for the future. Archie has mentioned the same thing recently."

"What do we do now then?" Eve asked. "I suppose we'll have to dispose of the skull now."

"We'll do no such thing!" May said with no little indignation.

"Calm, down, Ma." Sid said coming to his wife's rescue. "You clearly thought I'd told Eve who the skull belongs to. Or I should say, did."

Eve looked quickly from Sid to May, and then back to Sid again."

"Tell me what?" She said.

May turned to Eve again and tried to explain to her as best she could.

"I brought the skull back from France when I was out there looking for John." She began. "I just knew it had to be either John or Tom, his best mate in the war though I've never been a hundred percent sure which one. Oh, I've wished it was John's so many times so that I could lay his ghost to rest but I just couldn't prove it.

Anyway last night, as Billy was coming around, I heard him shout out *Tom* and he drew his left hand away from whatever it was that was troubling him. I think it could have been a bullet wound."

Eve looked puzzled.

"It's all here in John's final letter." May continued. "Look."

She drew a crumpled tear-stained letter from the large pocket on her cardigan and handed it to Eve.

Eve read it.

My Darling May,

This, as always, could be the last time I write to you. To our knowledge everyone except me and Tom has been killed in the last battle to save a small town in France. When this bloody war is over and we are reunited I should like to visit with yourself and try and make some happy memories here instead of all this madness which surrounds us on a daily basis now.

The thought of your warm embrace and Tom's wickedly dark sense of humour are the only things keeping me alive right now. I have a small cut to my left hand from a Jerry rifle bullet but nothing for you to worry about.

I met a convoy the other day. One of the men had a cap off a German soldier he met on Christmas Day at the football match. Frightfully nice chap the German was, he said. The Jerry's name was Henry, would you believe!

Hope the twins are behaving themselves and not giving you the run around too much. Give them a kiss from their daddy.

Anyhow. Love as always. You are all constantly in my thoughts.

John x

Eve couldn't believe the connections that were unravelling before her. But somehow, it all seemed so plausible.

"How did you know, Sid?" She asked looking at him questioningly. "How did you know about this connection between your dad and the skull?

"Well, I didn't really?" Sid answered. "Oh, I knew about the skull alright but not about who it could be. Then I found the letter under the cabinet over there when I dropped the cloth I used to clean my binoculars. It was there just peeping out. I picked it up and read it. Then all the commotion outside started."

"I mislaid that letter months ago." May explained. "I must have cleaned around that cabinet on dozens of occasions so I don't know how it could have got there or how I missed it."

May sounded a bit curt as she finished, concerned that Eve might think that she wasn't in the habit of doing much cleaning around the cottage.

As the conversation drew to a close, May went to the front door and pulled on her hat, coat and wellington boots. She decided that she needed to get to the tool shed and hide the skull good and proper this time.

As she opened the door she turned and spoke to Sid and Eve.

"I have to go out for a while. I don't know what time I shall be back so don't wait up for me."

Without another word she slipped quickly through the door and into the porch, shutting it quietly behind her. She struggled with the sliding porch door which was always stiff to open during the winter as the damp air made the wood swell. Having developed a technique of lifting and pulling over the years, May slid it open enough to slip through into the curtain of the night.

May was keen to re-hide the skull as soon as possible and she made her way into the garden with only the odd rustle of a hedgehog in the leaves or the hoot of an owl to keep her company.

Occasionally the moonlight would filter its way through the cloud and light up the ghostly objects below; revealing at least one of them to be an old rotten tree stump. It was covered in ferns and moss which had taken up residence after the old tree had been blown down in one of England's infamous storms.

May rounded the corner of the crazy paved path with several thoughts of where she could hide the skull passing through her mind. She scoured the grounds for several hours until she had made up her mind. She then collected the skull from the tool shed and hid it. While she did so, she found herself talking to it; telling it about Billy.

May carefully covered the skull then made her way back through the cottage garden. She and John had spent hours tending to the plants and shrubs. Between them they knew every square inch and nowhere else did she feel as close to him as she did there.

Time had passed by quickly and there was a faint hint of the dawn sky slowly marching over the horizon. Quietly she slipped back into the cottage and made her way to her bedroom. Swiftly undressing and getting into her night gown she snuggled into the warmth of her bed. It wasn't long before the sheets were slowly rising and falling and the silence of the room broken by the gentle snoring of the now sleeping and content May.

Chapter 16

Where, When and How

A shaft of bright light streaming through the gap in the curtains was waiting to get the boys when they drearily peeled their eyes open. Their sleep had been heavy and they both looked up at each other, squinting. Blurry eyed, Archie looked hard at Billy.

"Sandman got you too, eh?"

"Looks like it." Said Billy rubbing his eyes.

The boys pulled themselves up; both revealing different hairstyles though both resembled being dragged through a hedge backwards. They looked at the clock on the bedside cabinet which revealed the time to be seven thirty.

"Sunday." Archie blurted out.

He sat there for a second or two before suddenly bolting upright.

"THE SKULL!" He shouted out in a loud voice.

"Shhhh!" Billy whispered putting his finger to his lips and looking startled and stopping his cousin in his tracks.

Archie looked suitably guilty and put his hand to his mouth.

"I think Granny May knows about the skull." Billy said looking concerned. "I can't be sure but I'm convinced she does."

"How would she know about it?" Archie retorted.

"I don't know." Billy replied. "But all I know is she's been giving me funny looks as if she knows something. The last thing we want is for the skull to start 'moving around'."

"Oh yeah?" Archie laughed. "What does it do? Grow bony legs as if by magic?"

"It's true!" Billy said getting quite annoyed that Archie was doubting him. "You go and look in the tool shed after breakfast and you'll see."

The boys performed their morning race to the bathroom nearly knocking Uncle Sid over in the process.

"Steady boys!" He laughed. "See you at breakfast."

This was a shock to the boys as Uncle Sid's usual response was to scold them for running about in the cottage.

At breakfast the two boys discovered why they had not been yelled at for running. Uncle Sid was just glad to see that they were both alright after the excitement of the previous day.

Granny May appeared in the kitchen doorway with the usual mountain of toast in one hand and her brown teapot in the other.

"Sid's going to take you on a mystery tour today." She announced. "We'll pack you some lunch and all will be revealed later."

The boys gazed at each other in amazement. What could be so important that Sid was going to take them out? The two boys were usually left to make their own entertainment.

After wolfing down their breakfast faster than a steam train the two boys were told that they were being allowed to skip chores that morning. They cleaned their teeth and threw on their boots and coats. By the time they returned to the kitchen Granny May and Auntie Eve had pulled together a picnic feast fit for a king. Uncle Sid joined them carrying his binoculars and his trusty walking stick.

"You two reprobates ready then?" He asked with a mock look of seriousness on his face.

The two boys gave him a resounding *yes* and the three of them trudged out of the house and were about to start off down the driveway when Billy suddenly realised something. He ran back into the cottage and seconds later he emerged with his brand new binoculars that Granny May had bought him for his birthday.

"Are we ready now then?" Uncle Sid enquired raising his eyebrows at Billy.

Billy nodded.

Billy and Archie both blushed as they were both kissed in front of the other by Granny May.

The three adventurers set off in single file down the driveway while Aunt Eve and Granny May stood waving them off.

"Look after Sid for us!" The two ladies shouted after them, laughing.

Uncle Sid raised his hand in acknowledgement without turning, oblivious to the friendly jibe the ladies had made. As they rounded the corner by the large hedge bordering the left hand side of the driveway, Billy and Archie were not aware that they were setting of on another adventure that would be beyond their wildest dreams.

Still perplexed as to where their adventure would take them the two boys began to pluck up the courage to start asking Uncle Sid what they hoped were the right questions.

"Time for lunch yet?" Archie blurted out.

"Lunch?" Uncle Sid bellowed out with a raucous laugh. "You've only just had your breakfast, lad!"

Billy looked incredulously at Archie who just shrugged his shoulders as if to say he didn't see what the problem was. Billy shook his head.

"It's only nine o'clock!" He whispered to Archie understanding his uncle's outburst towards his cousin.

"How do you know that?" Archie said looking warily at Billy

Billy explained that he could gauge the time by looking at the position of the sun; a technique he had read about in one of his war books that covered the art of survival. Archie was just about to make some derogatory comment when Uncle Sid piped up.

"It's only nine o'clock, boys. We've got the whole day ahead of us yet."

Billy gave Archie a smug look which got him a playful thump on the arm from his cousin.

"Come on, you two!" Sid said taking a deep breath. "Keep up!"

With a purposeful stride he briskly strolled on. Archie had never seen his dad like this before and he wasn't ashamed to admit how it filled him with a little pride.

The three of them left the driveway and then climbed the old iron railings that were now to the left of them separating the road from the old wood that ran alongside it. Once over they went into the trees.

As they passed through the oaks, rowans and silver birches Uncle Sid stopped dead in his tracks.

"This is where it begins, boys." He announced looking excited.

"Where what begins?" The two boys answered in unison.

"Well, now you're old enough," Uncle Sid began, "we decided last night after you had gone to sleep that now was probably the time to tell you where, when and how the skull came to be here at Granny May's."

The boys' jaws dropped. They were stunned. Uncle Sid had known about the skull all along.

"How did you find it?"

"Where did it come from?"

"Who's was it?"

The questions came thick and fast at Uncle Sid. The boys could barely breath properly they were talking so fast. The whole situation had left them bristling with excitement that, in truth, could only be rivalled by how they felt on Christmas Eve.

"All in good time." Uncle Sid said holding his hands up to stop the torrent of questions. "What's the rush? All will be revealed in good time. I will, however, take you to where I discovered something that I think you will both be interested in."

"The skull!" The boys yelled out in unison and stared at each other.

In the meantime, Uncle Sid had started to march on ahead through the ferns and trees.

"Come on soldiers!" He cried out.

Billy and Archie scurried up to him as quickly as they could.

It seemed to be taking forever. It was as if time had stood still. They passed through some barbed wire fences and down a hill. The time had moved on an hour or more when, all of a sudden, Uncle Sid stopped. The two boys behind him were too close to him and were too busy whispering and wondering what was going to happen to see him stop. They walked right into him.

"Whoa, watch what you're doing!!" He cried out. "Mind you, I suppose you're still full of questions and excitement, aren't you?"

The two boys nodded.

"Can we eat anything yet?" Billy asked, the excitement and march through the woods having made him hungry now.

"All in good time." Uncle Sid said again making Billy wonder when, exactly, this good time was going to be.

"How much further, dad?" Archie's voice asked from the rear.

Uncle Sid looked hard at the boys. They had come quite a long way.

"No further." He said turning to the boys. "This is it. This is the spot!"

Uncle Sid bent down, his backpack just sliding enough to knock him on the back of his head. He wasn't fazed by this. Reaching down he pulled back some of the old brown bracken carpeting the ground revealing an old frame. Billy thought he recognised the old rivets that pitted the grey metal.

"I've seen that before." Billy said.

"Not this one, you haven't." Uncle Sid replied.

"What is it?" Archie asked with a curious look on his face.

"It's the canopy from a Lancaster bomber." Billy said excitedly. "I've seen one in my war book."

"That's right, Billy." Uncle Sid said grinning. "I found this as a boy on one of my adventures in the woods and used to come here often and pretend to be a pilot carrying out dangerous bombing missions."

Billy and Archie stared at Sid in amazement as they felt a connection to him they had not had before.

"Anyway, let's set the picnic up and I'll tell you all about how Granny May came to be in possession of the skull." Sid said.

Billy and Archie didn't know whether they preferred to eat or get straight to the heart of the mystery. A growl from Archie's stomach decided which way the battle was to go and before long the three of them were sat on the floor next to the canopy tucking into the picnic Granny May and Auntie Eve had prepared for them earlier.

Between mouthfuls of food, Uncle Sid began Granny May's story.

Chapter 17

May Goes to France

May stood alone. Her blonde hair had darkened in the rain and was now dripping water onto her coat. She shivered as the driving wind cut straight through to the bone. All around there was the usual hustle and bustle of any harbour. May had disembarked into an alien world.

She had only ever been over the county border to Shropshire and that was as a child. She remembered her father had just acquired a car and he took them all out for the day. What an adventure that was and here she was on another.

A few barrow boys passed by nearly knocking her over as her mind slowly unraveled to the immediate situation. Sacks and bricks; wood and rope; it all came off the boat. She was just glad the trip from Dover to Calais was over. The sea had been rough and tossed the boat from side to side and up and down with the waves crashing over the bow of the ship. All she could do was hang on to a length of rope which hung from the beam above her makeshift bed of crates and old moth-eaten grey woolen blankets which made her itch when she pulled them up closer to try and fend the cold off. The other thing she had to cling to was hope; the hope that one day she would be reunited with her husband who, as was written on the telegram she received back in England, was lost in action in 1941.

The rain was persistent and at times harder than others. May's dress was sodden and clung to her legs as she began the slow walk to what would be a new life.

She made her way uphill as most harbour towns sat high up above the water's edge. Hunger and thirst was now setting in.

There were a few cafes about the town which May noted were quaint; some with flowers; some with dogs tied outside the entrance looking bedraggled in the rain.

She almost tripped over the short man in his black and white outfit. She quickly apologised and the man instantly recognised her English accent. After a long pause and May staring into infinity in the deep blue eyes which were now fixated back at her the waiter spoke in a soft voice.

"Café, Mademoiselle?"

"Yes. I know it's a café." May retorted.

"Non, Mademoiselle. Café."

This time he raised his hand to his mouth and made an action that resembled drinking.

"Oh, I'm so sorry. Yes, well, tea if you have any."

"But of course." The waiter beamed back at her and held the door open for her as her bags clattered through the café.

The other customers stopped what they were doing and stared at the beautiful but bedraggled sight which had now apparently graced their town.

A few more moments of silence and study of the English woman and then slowly the hum of French conversation started up again; naturally talking about the stranger.

May sat down at a table for two carefully placing her bags up against the wall and settled in for her tea which was now steaming in front of her. The café appeared to be busier than when she had entered. Maybe word was spreading about the rain-soaked English woman.

May decided this was possibly a good thing as the more people who knew she was there, the better. After all she had questions – and lots of them. Maybe someone here knew about her husband.

Yet again she was snapped abruptly out of her thoughts by the waiter who had served all the other eager customers.

"May I ask what Madame's business is in France?"

May had noted the kindly look in the man's eyes and the soft tone of his voice.

"No time like the present." She muttered under her breath.

"Sorry, Madame?"

"Oh, nothing. I am here to hopefully discover what happened to my husband in the war. He was lost in action, you see. I am going to stay in France for a while until I find out the truth."

"Ah, you are renting Jacques cottage, no?"

"Yes. I mean, *Oui.* Jacque's barn. Could you point me in the right direction as I am a little tired from the journey and am in need of some rest?"

Henri stood there for a moment rubbing his chin, obviously thinking something through. After a while he folded his arms, nodded as if he'd come to some agreement with himself and then began to speak.

"If Madame can wait while I speak to my staff I would be more than happy to take you to the barn."

May shook her head slowly and smiled.

"That is very kind of you but I couldn't possibly put you to so much trouble."

"I insist." Henri said and, as if to close the matter, turned and went to speak to the waitress behind the counter.

After a brief exchange in French which included a little pointing in May's direction, the waiter returned with a smile.

"It is arranged then." He announced. "I will drive you over to Jacques' barn."

Before May had time to object further he removed his apron and walked towards the door. May gathered up her things and quickly followed him out to his car.

The ride in the grey ram-shackled Citroen 2CV, which was originally built for the French farmer hence the out of control suspension, was not in the least dignified. They had to stop at one point to retrieve May's straw hat after it had been sucked out of the window. Her long blonde hair had cascaded down her shoulders and May had blushed when Henri, who was a little younger than May, commented on how beautiful she had looked forcing her to look away. Henri seemed unaffected by her embarrassment and kept merrily feeding May information about the local surroundings whilst constantly taking his eyes off the road and his hands off the wheel.

After what seemed to be an eternity around the winding country lanes and an old looking dwelling loomed up at them around the final bend. Its distinctive red tiles and partly rendered walls, which were either not completed due to the war or were just unkempt, were typical of a few countries in Europe.

Henri slowly entered the driveway to the farm and pulled up at the door.

"Madame, your new home." He quipped while at the same moment smiling with his entire face and providing yet more gesticulating with his hands.

May had noticed on arrival there was a small coppice of trees to the north of the house and that there was a listless mound under one of the trees. She turned to Henri, touched the back of his hand, and asked what it was.

"Madame, it is *un chien* – a dog." He said.

"Is he friendly?" Was the most obvious thing to ask in May's eyes.

"*Oui, absolut.*" Henri replied.

"What is his name?" May continued.

She could not have guessed what was coming next. In fact, it completely took the wind out of her.

"*Bruno.*" Henri informed her in his distinctive husky, French voice. "His name is Bruno."

The name ricocheted through May's mind and she froze for a second or two.

"Is Madame alright?" Henri asked seeing the look of shock on May's face.

"Yes. Madame is… I mean… I am alright. Thank you."
May managed to say.

Unbeknown to Henri, Bruno was the nickname of John's
eldest brother who was tragically taken away from them in a
cricket accident. The ball had hit him square in the forehead;
and just as he was on the verge of scoring his first century for
the local village team of Gayton. The last words he was to
hear were those of the portly local vicar, who happened to be
at the other end of the cricket square, as he cradled Bruno's
head in his hands.

"Bad luck, old boy!" He'd choked and with that, Bruno
made his exit to the pavilion in the sky.

May did not want to go into detail right at that moment.
The journey was now taking its toll on her as tiredness began
to draw a veil over her eyes; not to mention the emotional
sledgehammer of old memories being brought to the fore by
the name Bruno.

Henri, being good at reading people's emotions, saw the
foundations of sleep weighing down on May.

"*Madame et dorma*?" He asked, then continued in
fragmented English he had part learnt from school and part
from the English soldiers in the war. "A bed awaits."

"What are you suggesting?" May said indignantly, getting
completely the wrong idea as to his meaning. "I'm not that
kind of woman!"

Henri laughed and mimicked sleep with his too hands.
May felt too embarrassed to speak so she just nodded.

The waiter got out of the car, walked around to May's
side and opened the door for her. She stepped out and slowly
made her way up the steps to the large farmhouse door. Henri
hurriedly lifted the cases out of the boot and looked up the
steps to May.

"Open the door, Madame." He said in his broken English.
"I will bring up the cases to your room. It is the second on
the left up the stairs."

Before she knew it she was in her room. However, on her way up she couldn't help but notice the tiled floor and sparse décor of the old house. There were signs of damp in the corner of the ceiling and a distinct smell of animals which filled the air. However, she found this was not entirely offensive to her nostrils as she had got chickens and pigs back in England.

In the war, everyone that owned land had to do their bit for the war effort and with around an acre May had enough room to provide pork, chicken, vegetables, honey, and fruit for her small hamlet in exchange for cakes, odd jobs and anything else she was in short supply of.

Over the next few days May got her bearings and had explored every last inch of the farm. On the third morning she sat with Bruno under the tree, as she had done on the previous two days. However this morning was different.

May had decided to wear one of John's old shirts and as she sat down next to Bruno his behaviour became a little erratic. His nose was twitching with more urgency and he kept standing up, sitting down and generally acting restless.

"What's wrong with you, Bru?" May laughed girlishly at him

Bruno had come to life and was acting like a puppy despite the fact he had been a part of the farm for a number of years now; something May had picked up from the milk man at the bottom of the drive the previous morning.

Bruno started to paw at the ground then ran down to the edge of the copse. He stopped, turned to look at May and started barking enthusiastically at her. May sat under the tree and watched with intrigue at the strange antics of the dog. It was as if he was trying to tell her something.

Bruno ran back to her and nudged her legs before running back down to the copse where he stopped, looked back and barked at her again.

"What's the matter, Bruno?" May shouted down to him.

She stood up and took a few steps towards him.

Bruno barked excitedly again and then disappeared amongst the trees.

Ok." May muttered to herself. "You want me to follow you, eh?"

She covered the distance to where Bruno had entered the trees briskly and followed the erratic barking into the copse.

For a while May could not see where Bruno was. All she had to guide her were his enthusiastic barks which emanated from the foliage in front of her. At one stage they seemed to get distant as Bruno, used to the narrow paths within the trees, quickly moved amongst them. Just when she thought she had lost the dog she came upon a clearing and found him there, sitting expectantly and frantically wagging his tail. On seeing May emerge into the clearing he started frantically digging at the ground.

May walked over to Bruno and patted his shoulders.

"What you found there, Bru?" She said.

Bruno had already dug at least a foot into the soft soil and was scooping it back through his hind legs as if his life depended on it. May could only watch on in awe as the canine digging machine excavated the earth from beneath him.

Suddenly, he stopped and sat down. He looked up to the sky and howled.

May looked down into the hole Bruno had dug and to her astonishment saw the tell-tale signs of bone sticking out of the soil. She dropped to her knees and gently brushed the surrounding dirt from around the cold, grey bone. She suddenly sat back onto the ground as it became apparent that what Bruno had uncovered was a skull!

Chapter 18

Finale

"So Granny May, with the help of her new found canine friend called Bruno, discovered the skull in the depths of a copse in France." Uncle Sid said to the two open mouthed boys sitting in front of him hanging on his every word. "She returned to the wood shed and found a trowel with which she was able to carefully dig it up. She put it in a box and carefully packed it with straw and then smuggled it back into England when she gave up her search for your granddad."

The two boys stared back at Uncle Sid wide-eyed.

"She smuggled it back into England!" Billy gasped. "Granny May!"

The thought of his grey-haired Granny as a smuggler astonished him. Granny May, who was always telling him he had to be good and respect the law! At this thought he let out a hearty laugh.

"Good old Granny May, I say!" He said.

"Anyway." Uncle Sid said not wanting to dwell too much on the illegalities of Granny May's exploits. "Granny may managed to bring the skull home where she hid it in the toolshed and that is where it has lain undiscovered until someone recently discovered it."

Uncle Sid looked across at Billy who could not contain his excitement any longer.

"Yes! Yes! It was me." He cried out. "I found it the other day in the shed when the boxes toppled over and it fell out and then I picked it up and …."

"Whoa!" Uncle Sid said holding his hands up in the air to slow Billy's excited outburst down. "All very exciting I'm sure. But now the skull has been found and you know how it came to be here. Anything else you know about it is probably best kept secret."

Billy stopped in mid-sentence and nodded. After all, who would believe him if he was to tell of his adventures.

"That's agreed then." Uncle Sid said looking first at Billy and then at Archie." Right, time is moving on and so should we. Let's get this picnic packed up and get on our way back. Granny May and Auntie Eve will be wondering where we are."

The two boys packed everything away while Uncle Sid inspected the canopy, lost in his own childhood adventures. Before long they were traipsing back through the wood. Back to Granny May's cottage and the promise of teatime!

Chapter 19

Remembrance

Billy stood next to Granny May as they looked at the names on the plaque.

Smith, Leech, Parker, Bentley ...

They were all men who had given their lives in the war defending their country and trying to make a difference.

Along from the list of those killed in action was another ageing plaque with LIA inscribed at the top of it.

"What is LIA?" Granny May asked.

"Lost In Action." Billy replied solemnly.

Granny May's shoulders drooped a little before she wandered over to it. There was a large story board in front which she began to read. As she did so tears began to run down her cheeks and Billy put his arm around her; feeling her frail body tremble against him.

Billy was not long turned sixteen and it was his first day at military camp; a day he would have been late for had he not suddenly noticed the time at Granny May's and quickly got himself ready. He had taken some time to take a last look around the grounds. At one stage he had found himself sitting on the cold garden wall that was slowly crumbling away thanks to the ever-changing English weather and from where Billy and Archie had re-enacted their war games.. He had been too busy mulling over his short life and the adventures he'd had with the skull. A smile had crept across his face as he thought about how he was following in his granddad John's footsteps and his heart swelled with pride.

Standing there now, at the story board, he was unaware that he was about to relive some of those adventures again.

Billy began to read the stories that were presented before him. To his amazement he found himself reading about his adventures. Some of the names of the people he'd met in them were there. Even Mad Mick featured! Billy couldn't believe what he was reading. This was the Lost in Action section. How on earth could they have known about him?

Billy held Granny May's hand and looked into her tear stained face.

"John?" They both said together.

Their world turned on its head and, not for the first time, questions came rushing into them; the biggest being *How?*

A few feet away from them an elderly man had been standing with his grandson and was also taking in the memorials on the wall. As Granny May and Billy had called out John's name he had lifted his head and started to walk towards them. As he approached he cleared his throat.

"Excuse me." He said speaking with a slight quiver in his voice. "I hope you don't mind me interrupting you but I heard you shout the name John."

Granny May looked up at the tall, dignified man in front of her and smiled proudly.

"Yes." She said. "John was my husband and Billy's Granddad."

She nodded towards Billy.

"Pleased to meet you." Billy said thrusting out his hand.

The old man took Billy's hand and shook it, not displeased at the firm grip Billy returned.

"Good strong handshake, son." He announced. "I like that. Shows confidence."

Billy took in the man in front of him. He looked around Granny May's age; the lines on his face deep. Despite a pronounced furrowed brow that betrayed the fact that he had seen more than any man should be asked to see, the old man still had a twinkle in his eyes that Billy thought was almost roguish.

The old man was obviously a soldier; a fact given away by his beret and matching green jacket. He had a chest full of medals that hung proudly in a row and that were, like his boots, highly polished with love. Despite his age, the man stood straight backed, tall and proud.

"You must have been an easy target with all those pinned on your chest." Billy said smiling cheekily but not meaning to cause offence. "How on earth did you make it through?"

"Billy!" Granny May said looking horrified and reprimanded him with a slap to the shoulder.

"It's alright." The old man said laughing and shaking his head slowly. "I like a man with a sense of humour too. No offence taken."

Billy was just about to start his interrogation of the old man when Granny May, turning her attention to the younger man, headed him off.

"And who might this young gentleman be?" She asked.

"This is my grandson Henry." The old man announced puffing his chest out and placing his hand on Henry's shoulder. "He's joining the army and this is his first day at camp."

Billy was just about to say that it was his first day too but the old man carried on.

"Now then. Back to the matter at hand." He said pointing to the memorials. "You mentioned someone called John. I knew a John back in 1941. We met over in France and very quickly became friends."

He stopped what he was saying rather abruptly and stood staring at May for a moment.

"It's very strange but I feel I should know you." He continued looking puzzled.

"I don't remember ever meeting you before." Granny May said shaking her head.

"Can I ask what your name is?" The old man asked Granny May smiled.

"Of course you can. My name is May."

The old man immediately went cold and the blood drained from his face as it raced to his vital organs to stop them from going into shock. Granny May placed her hands on his shoulders and shook him gently, not really realising what she was doing.

"What's wrong?" She said sounding concerned. "You look like you've seen a ghost."

"Granddad?" Henry said looking worried. "Are you alright? Do you need to sit down?"

The old man seemed lost for words and just stood there staring at May.

"What's this all about?" May said starting to feel a mixture of anger with the stranger in front of her despite her concern for him. "Just exactly who are you?"

The old man seemed to snap out of his daze.

"Tom!" He said. "My name's Tom. And I think I knew your husband!"

May felt dazed. So dazed that she was having difficulty comprehending what was happening. Surely this was all a coincidence and this Tom knew another John. Not her John.

Tom could see the doubt on her face and thought hard how he could prove one way or the other that they were both talking about the same John.

"The letter!" He suddenly cried out. "I sent my John's May a letter he'd written."

This time it was May's turn to feel light headed. Billy gently put his arm around her and went to lead her away but May stood firm, the colour rushing back to her cheeks.

"I received a letter from him just after the war." She told Tom. "It was what made me think he may still be alive. It was the letter that gave me the strength to go to France to look for him."

May saw the relief on Tom's face when he realised that he'd convinced her that he knew John; relief that was slowly replaced by sadness. Slowly, it dawned on her. She stood up straight and took a deep breath.

"John's dead isn't he?"

Tom nodded slowly.

"I'm sorry I can't give you good news, May." Tom said and he took May's hand gently in his.

"Were you with him?" May asked. "When he died?"

Tom nodded again.

May felt like she had a million and one questions to ask Tom; all about John and all about laying his ghost to rest.

"What happened?" She asked.

Tom thought for a moment before he spoke.

"This probably sounds a little presumptuous but can I perhaps buy you a drink?" He said kindly. "There's a coffee shop attached to the regiment museum. Maybe we could go and get a tea or something. And while we do, I'll tell you everything."

May smiled solemnly and nodded.

Billy took his Granny May in his arms and gave her a hug. "You alright?" He asked.

"You're a good lad, Billy." Granny May said. "And I'm fine. Now, it seems, I get to find out what really happened to your granddad."

Billy bent down and Granny May kissed him on the cheek.

"You're welcome to join us if you want, lad." Tom said

Billy shook his head.

"Thanks but I think I'll hang around with Henry here for a while if that's ok?" He said.

Tom looked at Henry who smiled and made a shooing motion with his hands.

"Go, Granddad." He said. "Me and Billy can get to know each other as it seems we're joining up together."

Tom made a loop with his arm and May slipped hers through it. Together they set off slowly towards the coffee shop.

"You can still go with them if you want." Henry said. "Granddad tells a mean war story."

"Nah, it's ok." Billy replied. "I don't think somehow he could tell any tale I haven't already experienced."

Henry looked puzzled at Billy.

"Don't worry." Billy said. "If we're going to be mates, and I somehow think we're destined to, then I might just tell you one or two tales of my own."

With that, Billy gave Henry a friendly slap on the back and the two new recruits continued there exploration of the memorials.

Epilogue – Tom's Story

May sat at the first available table while Tom went to the counter and ordered coffee for them both. When he returned, he placed a cup in front of her and then sat down. As she sipped her coffee, Tom recounted the story of how he and John first met in the war.

A Shot in the Dark

John gripped his rifle. His fingers were almost white as the blood left them and coursed through his veins to other vital parts of his body. His heart was pounding and he struggled to keep his breathing slow and quiet.

Another twig snapped somewhere close behind him. John spun round on one heal.

"Reveal yourself, you coward!" He called into the dark.

As his eyes focused on the darkness of the wood he saw the movement of an animal. He gave out a sigh of relief. He was just about calming down and smiling to himself when a familiar and disturbing sound resonated through the still of the night. It was the tell-tale sound of a gun being cocked!

This time John spun around and began firing erratically through the trees.

"Hey! Don't shoot. Me gun won't cock properly. That's not a fair fight!" A startled voice yelled from the blackness of the surrounding woodland.

John stopped firing and, uncontrollably, words cascaded from his mouth in the direction of the loan voice.

"English! You're English!" He called out as relief set in.

At that, a well set rugged man revealed himself as he walked slowly towards him.

"Name and rank?" John demanded with a not to subtle hint of confidence in his voice.

The soldier now stood close enough to him for him to look up to as John himself was not the largest in stature.

"Geddins, Tom; Staffordshire 2nd Regiment; Corporal 203479, Sarge." The soldier fired back looking down at John with the same degree of confidence whilst at the same time he snapped the heels of his boots together and raised his hand to his head to give John a friendly salute.

"Where's the rest of your command?" John asked with the hint of a smile and a quizzical look on his face.

"I could ask the same of you, sir. And just for the record what's your name and number?" Tom said looking slightly perplexed himself.

John was caught off guard with the question that had been fired at him and answered far too quickly.

"Steadman, John; Staffordshire 1st regiment; acting Sargent 20297."

Just as John finished giving his rank and number there was a succession of distant gunfire which had the two soldiers scanning the surrounding area.

John, as the senior officer of the two, took immediate charge of the situation.

"We better get a move on and try to link up with the rest of the regiment." He said. "I don't fancy the two of us getting caught out here alone by those Jerries. Last I heard the Seventh Panzer division was closing in on this area."

Tom, always up for a fight no matter what the odds, looked forlornly towards where the gunfire had originated from and reluctantly bowed down to John's command.

As the air became cold and the shadows of the night crept endlessly through the trees, John and Tom made their way stealthily through the dense woodland in the hope of finding some short respite from the advancing enemy. Every now and then the two new acquaintances would stop simultaneously and listen for some clue as to what direction the enemy might be coming from. But all they got was the faint grind of the heavy artillery tracks as they devoured the countryside beneath them.

"Bloody Panzers!" John blurted out.

"They'll get what's coming to them." Tom quickly answered back.

Tom felt a strange sense of curiosity towards John, particularly as he seemed so calm and collected given the situation they were in. This calmness was in stark contrast to Tom's eagerness to take the fight to the enemy.

"You've been in this war too long, mate!" He said to his new comrade.

John looked thoughtful for a moment.

"Missing my girl terribly so I must have been." He returned. "Mind you, soon be time to go home one way or another."

"Hang on there, mate!" Tom said shaking his head. "I don't know about you but I've every intention of getting out of this alive. Pie and a pint at the local back in Blighty for you and me when we get out of here."

John sighed and nodded.

"You're right." He said as they continued their journey. "It's just that I find it hard to stay positive knowing that my family are back home worrying about me."

Tom laid a hand on John's shoulder and was just about to offer him some uncharacteristic words of comfort when a voice bellowed at them from a clearing ahead.

"Where the blazes have you been!"

Standing there was Tom's Sargent-Major, looking as uncompromising as ever. Tom's shoulders dropped as the two comrades were re-united with his unit.

*

"So now you know how we met." Tom said lifting his cup to his lips and taking a swig of his own coffee. "We were big mates from that moment on, even though John was a higher rank than me."

"That was John all over." May said staring wistfully in front of her. "No airs or graces. Never thought of himself as better than anyone else."

She went quiet for a moment carefully considering her next question; the question that had been on her mind ever since that fateful telegram ripped her life apart.

"Were you with John when he …" She hesitated for a moment. Now that it seemed she was about to know the truth the words seemed to fail her.

Tom sadly nodded.

"I need to know." She finally said. "I need to know what happened to John in his final days."

Tom took a deep breath and solemnly continued.

On the Run

Tom reached the edge of the clearing and stood there panting. He reached out to rest his free hand against the trunk of a sturdy tree as his breath vented forth like the steam billowing out from the funnel of one of the trains he used to love to watch when he was a boy. The early morning air had been chilled by the frost and felt like a thousand ice daggers piercing his windpipe as he tried to fill his lungs.

Tom had been supporting John for the last few miles. His injured colleague was slumped over his shoulders unable to put any weight on his right leg which had been pierced by a ricocheting bullet as they had made their escape from the German patrol.

Tom stared down at John's trouser leg which was now soaked in blood. He feared that his friend had already lost too much. John seemed to read his mind and tried to push himself free of Tom's grasp.

"Leave … me… here…" He said through gritted teeth, the cold biting into his wound. "I'm only slowing you down."

Tom took a firmer grip of his friend.

"Oh no, you don't!" He whispered trying to make light of the situation. "You don't get to play hero on my watch. We're in this together, mate."

"But you can't carry me forever." John grimaced. "Those Jerries can't be too far behind us. You stand a better chance of out running them on your own so leave me."

"I'm not leaving you so you can just stop with all that nonsense talk."

As if to prove a point Tom stood away from the tree and readjusted John over his shoulder to take more of his weight. He looked at his friend with compassion before continuing.

"Besides, if I left you here who else would I be able to share my adventures with? You've got to admit it, mate, we've had our fair share over the time we've known each other."

John smiled and closed his eyes. When he opened them again he looked a little brighter.

"That's better." Tom said grinning. "Me and you are going to make it out of this war. We got more than enough stories to keep our grandchildren entertained for many a long winter's night. We'll have us a few more too before this wars over, you'll see."

John laughed but then a sharp pain fired from his wound and seemed to grip his whole body. It was all he could do not to scream. Tom held him tight trying to comfort him until the pain relented. Finally he felt John relax a little.

"You ok?" He asked.

John nodded slowly; his face contorted with pain; his eyes closed.

"Something tells me … this will be our last … adventure." He murmured between breaths as he slumped against Tom. "The pain … is getting worse. And I feel … so cold. My legs … are so numb … I can't feel … my feet."

"We need to find you somewhere warm to rest." Tom said quickly glancing around him and praying that they could find some sort of shelter soon.

John grimaced as another bolt of pain shot through him.

Tom desperately peered out of the woods and into the clearing. To his joy, he saw what looked like an old farmhouse about half a mile to his right.

"Yes!" He cheered under his breath.

He patted John gently on the shoulder.

"Hold on just a little longer, mate. I'll soon have you nice and cozy with your feet up."

He pulled John up further so that he could take as much of his friend's weight off his injured leg as possible and emerged into the clearing. Steadily they made their way towards the farmhouse in the distance.

Sanctuary

Whether it was the weight of carrying his friend or he had grossly underestimated the distance Tom felt he had travelled more than the half mile he'd calculated the farmhouse to be away. By the time they walked up the path to the door he felt totally exhausted. John was now beginning to drift in and out of consciousness. More worryingly, when he was conscious he was in a state of delirium. As they approached the door they were greeted by the excited puppy-like bark of a dog that seemed to be coming from one of the farm's outhouses nearby.

Tom gently lowered his friend onto a bench running along the left hand side of the porch outside the solid wood farmhouse door. He reached for the big metal knocker that hung three quarters of the way up it and wrapped it four times loudly; as much as his strength seemed to be able to cope with. He stood back.

No one came.

He waited for what seemed like an eternity before he tried again; louder this time.

Still no one came.

Tom thought he'd try and open the door but it was locked.

He tried a third time but with the same result.

To the right of the door was a paneled window. He stepped across, rubbed the dirt from one of the panes with his sleeve and then, cupping his hands, peered in.

From the window he found himself looking into what appeared to be the farmhouse kitchen. It was dark and at first glance seemed deserted. However, once his eyes adjusted he could make out the shapes of a man and woman huddled together at the back of the room. They were holding each other's arms and looked scared witless.

Tom wrapped on the glass.

"S'il vous plait monsieur, Madame ..." He began, the extent of his French exhausted as he realised he'd been in France all this time and not bothered to pick up the language.

"Please, my friend is injured and we need shelter."

The man in the kitchen suddenly became agitated and left the woman's side. He strode over to a long box on one of the walls and, to Tom's dismay, took out a shotgun.

Turning to face the soldier, he cocked the gun before slipping in two cartridges and snapping it shut again. He pointed it towards the window and waved the gun to indicate that Tom should go away.

"Allez! Allez!" He shouted at the window.

Tom could see the farmer was shaking and was concerned that the gun was likely to go off inadvertently at any moment. He stood away from the window and stepped back towards John. As he looked down on his friend he was alarmed to see how hot and sweaty John had become in such a short time. His eyes were closed and he was murmuring incoherently.

Tom picked him up and turned to walk away from the door. Their need for shelter was great but he was not prepared to get shot for it. He had taken a couple of steps down the path when he heard the door open behind him. He closed his eyes and hunched his shoulders as he waited for the blast to hit him. Instead he heard a soft voice calling out to him.

"Monsieur… Monsieur!"

Tom turned to look over his shoulder. The woman from the kitchen was standing in the doorway, the man behind her with his gun shouldered.

"Vite! Vite!" She called out beckoning him into the farmhouse.

Tom looked up at the man for confirmation. The two men stared at each other for a moment before the Frenchman, shame-faced, nodded and also beckoned him in. Tom stumbled in with John and staggered towards a large table. The Frenchman peered nervously out of the door and scanned quickly around him. Satisfied that there was no one else out there he closed the door and locked it.

The woman pulled out one of the chairs and Tom sat his friend on it. As he did so, the woman rushed to the sink and then brought back two glasses of water. He then remembered the only other two French words he had managed to learn.

"Merci!" He said gratefully. "Merci beaucoup!"

Stand-Off

The cold water had tasted like nectar to Tom as almost in one go he gulped it down. While the farmer's wife went back to the sink to refill the glass he tried to get John to drink. At first his friend refused to open his mouth. Gradually Tom managed to gently force a little water through his lips. The cool water seemed to have a galvanising effect on John. His eyes suddenly opened wide and he stared around the kitchen with the look of a madman. He screamed out a curse and, flailing his arms around, knocked the glass out of Tom's hand. Tom was caught off balance and as he sprawled backwards the glass bounced across the stone floor before hitting the far wall and shattering.

John leaped to his feet in a fever-induced rage only for his injured leg to cruelly crumple beneath him causing him to stagger forward. Unable to control his fall, his head hit the edge of the table with a sickening crack and he was knocked unconscious.

The woman ran back to Tom's aid and helped him to his feet whilst the man, becoming agitated again, brought both barrels of the shotgun to bear on John's prone body. If it hadn't been for his friend being out cold rendering him motionless, Tom believed any movement John would have made would have forced the farmer to shoot him there and then; such was the Frenchman's nervous state of mind.

"No, please!" Tom shouted out, his arms stretched in front of him as if he could hold back any impending discharge of the gun by sheer will power.

The Frenchman's eyes darted nervously from John to Tom and then back to John again. His hands were shaking and Tom expected him to pull the trigger at any moment.

Calmly, but swiftly, the woman left Tom's side and walked over to the man.

"Jacques!" She called out in a soothing voice. "Non! Il est mal." *He's ill.*

The man, Jacques, seemed confused as to what to do for a moment before deciding to lower the gun. The woman joined him and placed a loving hand on his arm.

"Merci, Madame! Merci" Tom whispered as he slowly walked over to his fallen friend, eager not to make any sudden movements that might antagonise the gun toting Frenchman, despite his wife having seemingly calmed him.

Tom gently picked John up and stood holding him in the middle of the kitchen; unsure what he was meant to do next. The woman looked across at him and then finally indicated that Tom should follow her. She walked over to a door that the soldier assumed must lead into the rest of the farmhouse and disappeared through it. Quickly, Tom followed.

Parting of the Ways

The woman led Tom deeper into the farmhouse. At the end of the corridor leading from the kitchen, she turned off left into another room. Tom followed her in.

The room had a solitary single bed in the middle of it. Behind it was a window with a deep bay. To one side was a wardrobe whilst to the other was an old leather chair. The woman quickly went to the bed and pulled back the covers. She indicated that Tom should lay John down. Tom obliged.

The woman mimed that Tom should start to remove his friends clothing. Tom nodded that he understood and began by taking off John's boots. The woman moved to leave the room but Tom gently grasped her arm.

"Merci." He said sincerely.

The woman nodded, her eyes large and compassionate.

"Tom." He added, pointing to himself.

The woman nodded again.

"Helene." The woman replied pointing to herself.

Tom smiled at her.

"John." He said pointing towards his friend.

Helene nodded gravely.

"Jacques?" He asked pointing towards the kitchen.

"Oui. Jacques." Helene replied nodding and raising her eyebrows as she did. "Mon Jacques!"

Tom could see by Helene's expression that she was trying to apologise for her husband's antics with the gun. He could also read in her eyes the deep love she had for him too. Tom smiled to let her know he understood and then released her arm. Helene disappeared out of the room.

Tom continued undressing John who was gradually starting to regain consciousness. He removed his friend's blood stained trousers and then his jacket. As he did so a small photograph fell out of John's top pocket along with an unopened letter. The photo was of a young girl, hardly older than nineteen Tom guessed. Her lush blonde curly hair encircled a beautiful face. Her eyes were sparkling and her lips were smiling. The letter was addressed to someone in England.

John had mentioned once that he was married though he didn't like to talk about the girl he had had to leave behind at home. On the one occasion he had got drunk and begun to open up about her the air raid siren had gone off and they had had to seek shelter from the falling bombs. However, by the end of it John had either forgotten what they had been previously talking about or, as was more likely, chosen to clam up again. Tom had not pushed him on the matter.

All Tom knew about John's wife was that her name was May. His friend had told him yet it was obvious to Tom that John didn't like to talk about her too much because that made him miss her more. If the picture was anything to go by Tom could understand why.

Tom put the photograph and letter into the back pocket of his trousers for safekeeping.

By the time Helene returned with a bowl of water, some towels and what looked like a make shift first aid kit, Tom had his friend stripped down to his underclothes and tucked into bed with just his injured leg protruding from the sheets. John's clothes were now piled up in a corner of the room and Tom had plonked himself down on the leather chair.

As Helene walked through the door Tom went to get out of the chair to help her. She gestured for him to stay seated and placed the bowl in the window. Tom collapsed back into the chair.

John was on fire as the fever from his wound gripped him. He was delirious and continuously murmuring gibberish. Helene placed a damp towel across his forehead and then turned her attention to his leg.

The soldier's long john's were caked in blood; both dried and fresh. Helene gently cut away the material around the wound and then gently pressed the flesh around it. Dark blood like sludge oozed up and out of it and John's mumblings increased in pitch.

Helene looked across at Tom; her face full of concern and sorrow. Slowly she shook her head at him leaving him in no doubt that his deepest fears for his friend were confirmed. The wound was mortal and there was nothing anyone could now do for him.

Helene cleaned around the wound with some hot water but was unable to stem the flow of blood. The bullet was too deeply buried in the muscle for her to retrieve but even if she could have dug it out of his leg, John was too weak to be able to sustain the resultant loss of blood. She bandaged it as best she could and tried to make John as comfortable as possible.

Tom felt bone-weary. The adrenalin that had allowed him to get his wounded friend this far was now rapidly ebbing away and all he really wanted to do was sleep. However, he fought the drowsiness, determined to stay awake for his friend. Helene recognised this and motioned to him that he should give in and get some sleep. She mimed that she would watch over John. Too weary to fight her Tom closed his eyes and fell asleep.

He didn't know how long he had been asleep when he felt himself being shaken awake. He had no idea what time it was but he guessed from his body clock that it must have been the early hours of the morning. He opened his eyes to find Helene's sad face looming over him. He looked across at

John. His eyes were closed and he looked peaceful. With no little hope he sat up and queried Helene with his eyes. But that hope was instantly quashed by a sad shake of her head.

"Il est mort." She said, a tear slowly running down her cheek.

Tom didn't need a translator to know his biggest fear had been realised. John was dead and he was now on his own.

Burial

Helene exited the room and left Tom alone with his friend. After all that they'd been through, he couldn't believe that John had actually gone. He knelt down by the side of the bed and, despite not being a religious man, said a small prayer over his friend's body.

He felt great sorrow at the loss of the man he had spent a great deal of the war fighting beside. However, his weariness seemed to put up a barrier to his ability to weep.

From his prone position by the bed he was suddenly aware of a presence in the doorway. He turned to find a solemn faced Jacques standing there. He had relinquished his gun and was now holding a spade to his chest.

"Monsieur?" The Frenchman said nodding at John's body and then holding the spade slightly in front of him.

Tom closed his eyes and nodded. Despite his grief he could see the sense in Jacques' eagerness to bury his friend as soon as possible. As sad as it seemed, they needed to lay him to rest before the following Germans arrived to find him. If that happened then Jacques and Helene would be in serious trouble for harbouring an enemy soldier. As it would also soon be daybreak burying John under the cover of dark seemed the sensible thing to do too.

Tom redressed John in his uniform, wrapped his body in the sheets off the bed and then gently lifted him over his shoulder. Jacques collected together the soldier's clothes and boots before leading Tom out of the room, down into the kitchen and through the back door.

The silence of the night was broken once more by the excited barking of the puppy in the outhouse. Jacques motioned for Tom to stay put while he went over and freed the excitable Labrador. It went straight over to the soldier and started sniffing his trousers before curiously sniffing the parcel Tom held over his shoulder.

"Bruno! Ici!" Jacques called out quietly and the dog obediently came to heal. Jacques nodded at Tom and they set off again.

The night sky was clear and Tom didn't think he had ever seen it filled with so many twinkling stars. The moon was full and shone down on the frosty landscape below it. Jacques indicated that Tom should follow him into the woods that lay behind the farmhouse. Tom obliged and the Frenchman led him deep into the trees, Bruno bounding off in front of them.

It took them nearly an hour to find a spot that Jacques was happy with. There was a small clearing and the Frenchman tapped the ground with his spade.

"Ici." He whispered.

Tom lay John's body gently on the ground while Jacques began to dig. The surface of the ground was quite hard thanks to the frost but, taking it in turns and working up quite a sweat in the process, they managed to dig a hole wide enough and deep enough to bury John in.

Tom gently picked up his friend's body and carefully laid him at the bottom of the trench. Jacques leaned on his spade watching while Tom finally put John to rest. When the soldier stood up and stepped back, the Frenchman crossed himself and then threw the first shovel full of dirt over John's body.

"Wait!" Tom called out and reached into his pocket.

Jacques obeyed with a grunt of dissatisfaction and then returned to leaning on the spade.

Tom pulled out the photograph of John's wife and then leaned down into the grave. With a little effort he managed to loosen the shroud and insert the picture next to John's chest, near to his now still heart. Standing up, he indicated that Jacques could now finish burying his friend.

It took them less than half the time to fill the grave than dig it and when finished, hid it as best they could with surrounding fallen branches and leaves. With a final sad nod of good-bye to his fallen comrade Tom turned and followed the Frenchman back out of the woods and towards the farmhouse.

Captured

Tom had lain low on the farm for a week or more. His heart was heavy from the burden of knowing there was nothing he could have done to save his friend's life.

Jacques and Helene had fed and watched over Tom with a close eye to make sure he did nothing to jeopardise the safe house which had been a sanctuary for many an allied soldier over the duration of the war so far.

Tom awoke in a cold sweat, sitting bolt upright in his bed. Only one option was left. At the break of dawn he would pack what few possessions he had and leave the good people that had been looking out for him to save them for falling prey to the wrath of the enemy. Tom knew that if they were caught harbouring Allied soldiers their punishment would be swift and hard. He lay his head back on the pillow and fell back into a fitful sleep.

Tom woke up again just as the light was inching its way through the moth eaten curtains hanging in the window.

Shouting and dogs barking from the south of the cottage were all he needed to force himself into action.

A voice broke the still air of the morning.

"Get down and be quiet!"

It was Jacques.

Unbeknown to Tom, Jacques had made an underground shelter and, as the smell that now emanated into his room attested to, the Frenchman had scattered rotting fish and vegetables all around the hut to throw the impending assault off the scent of any of the inhabitants; particularly Tom.

He quickly packed his bag but it was too late. As Tom ran through the house and out of the backdoor a large black boot struck his shin bringing him to the ground with a thump. As he lay there, he heard the tell-tale click of rifles being made ready, accompanied by the sound of hearty laughter. He looked up to see about a dozen rifle barrels pointing down at him.

"Der Englander must be tired!" One of the blue suited soldiers called out, much to the amusement of the group now staring down at him.

Tom cursed his luck. This was a major flaw in his escape plan. If only he had gotten out of there a day earlier. But it was no use thinking about what he should have done. What he needed to do now was ensure that his capture deflected his captors away from the search for Jacques and his wife; a search that one or two of the German soldiers were starting to begin.

The soldiers were joined by another in a smart suit and peaked cap; obviously their commander.

"Englander, do not attempt anything foolish. You are surrounded and are now a prisoner of war. As such, you will be treated accordingly as long as you co-operate fully."

"Bleedin' Germans!" Tom muttered under his breath.

"What did you say?" The commander said cocking his head and looking menacingly at Tom.

"I said, right you are." Tom answered quickly.

The commander glared at Tom for a moment and then pointed to one of the soldiers nearby.

"You, Otto, pick up this man and take him to the truck." He barked out his order. "And if he makes any funny business, shoot him."

Otto stepped forward and shouldered his rifle so he could help Tom to his feet. Tom was amazed at how young the soldier looked reckoning he could be no older than eighteen. The young soldier lifted him up out of the mud.

Having helped Tom to his feet Otto stepped back from him quickly. Tom took a step towards him and began to bend. Otto quickly unshouldered his rifle and pointed it at the British soldier. His hands were shaking a little and Tom quickly stood up straight with his hands up by his sides.

"My boot lace!" He said slowly nodding at the ground towards his footwear.

Otto quickly glanced at the ground and saw that the laces on Tom's right boot had come underdone, most probably when he had been tripped. Staring back at Tom the German nodded and indicated with his head that the British soldier could tie it.

Tom slowly bent down and secured his laces. Carefully he stood up again. Otto pointed his rifle at Tom's hands and indicated that he should put them up. Tom did as he was asked. Otto then quickly took his left hand from the rifle and placed it on his head, indicating that Tom should do the same. Tom obliged as Otto swiftly returned his hand to the gun. The young German soldier swept the rifle slightly to the left to tell Tom to start walking. With a sigh of resignation Tom started walking towards the front of the hut where a grey canvas covered truck with a black and white emblem on its door was waiting for him; Otto a safe distance behind, periodically poking his rifle into Tom's back to gee him up whilst not for one moment taking his eyes of his prisoner.

Tom climbed into the back of the truck and sat by the tailgate. Otto followed him up and sat opposite him, his hands still securely on his rifle. Tom calculated that he could quite easily overpower the youngster in front of him but to what avail? There were more than enough soldiers there to cut him down if he ran. So he sat there, resigned to his fate.

The commander appeared at the front of the house and was soon joined by the rest of his men. They were all shaking their heads and looking confused. The commander shook his head and then snarled out a command in German. The soldiers jumped at his command and quickly got themselves into their vehicles. The commander strode over to the back of the truck holding Tom and for a split second the British soldier feared the worst. However, the commander just glared at him and then secured the tailgate before disappearing to his staff car.

Tom suddenly realised he was holding his breath and so he gently let it out. If there was one good thing to come out of this disastrous situation it was that it didn't seem that Jacques and his wife had been found. He smiled to himself and sat back. As he did so he remembered the letter in his back pocket. Quickly he placed his went to retrieve it but found, to his dismay, that it was gone. With a heavy heart he sat back against the rough support of the seat.

Suddenly, the truck lurched forward and he was on his way to captivity.

"So I spent the rest of the war locked away in a prisoner-of-war camp." Tom said looking ruefully at May. "Oh, I tried to escape a number of times but was never successful. In the end I had to wait to be liberated by the army as they marched across France towards Germany. The German guards had deserted their posts by then so there was no resistance. We were all shipped back to England on the first available troopship and never saw any more action."

"The letter." May said looking puzzled. "It arrived not long after the war. How could that have been?"

"You received it?" Tom said looking puzzled. "But I thought it had been lost."

"It was that letter that gave me the hope that John might still be alive." May said. "It even had me going to France to search for him I was that convinced that he may have survived. How did it get to me?"

Tom shook his head.

"Someone must have found it." He said shrugging his shoulders. "Then posted it after the war. Maybe Jacques or Helene. I supposed we'll never know."

May thought about the skull back at the cottage finally convinced once and for all who it had belonged to. All this time she had been so close to John. But she realised she knew this anyway. Why else would circumstances conspire for her to find it?

May decided there and then that she would give the skull a proper burial the next time Billy was home from leave. She would invite Sid, Eve and Archie; even Billy's mum and his good-for-nothing father. But most of all she thought tom should be there too.

The thought of finally burying John filled her with mixed emotions of relief and sadness.   May looked at Tom with tears in her eyes.

"Thank you." She said. "Thank you for being with my John at the end. I've waited all these years to find out what happened to him and it's comforting to know that he was not alone when he died."

Tom's own eyes began to well up and May placed her hand on his as it lay on the table. It was comforting to know that here was someone else who cared for her John as deeply as she did.

"I've never forgotten him, you know." Tom said. "There's not a day goes by that he's not been in my thoughts. He was the best mate a soldier could have."

May felt a lump starting to form in her throat when she heard the familiar voice of her grandson call out to her from the doorway of the cafe.

"Come on Gran." Billy said smiling. "Me and Henry have got to get going."

May patted the back of Tom's hand and smiled.

"Let's go and get these two handed over to the military." She said. "Heaven only knows what mischief them two are going to get up to now they're being unleashed on the world."

"Oh, I think I know alright!" Tom laughed. "I think I know only too well!"

With that, Tom stood up, helped May to her feet and then led her towards the two eager young recruits standing expectantly outside the café.

Made in the USA
Charleston, SC
14 July 2014